THE IVORY PRINCESS

For historical illustrator Tanwen Jones, her new job at the site of a ruined abbey in North Wales is a dream come true. But, as she helps to uncover the tragic love story of a mediaeval noblewoman, she begins to realise that all is not well. With priceless artefacts from the dig mysteriously disappearing, Tani soon finds herself caught up in a perilous web of greed, treachery, and deceit. But who can she trust? And is it her life, or her heart, that is in the greatest danger . . . ?

Books by Heather Pardoe
in the Linford Romance Library:

HER SECRET GARDEN

HEATHER PARDOE

◆

THE IVORY PRINCESS

Complete and Unabridged

LINFORD
Leicester

First published in Great Britain in 2004

First Linford Edition
published 2005

British Library CIP Data

Pardoe, Heather
   The ivory princess.—Large print ed.—
Linford romance library
   1. Excavation (Archaeology)—Wales—Fiction
   2. Archaeological thefts—Fiction
   3. Love stories
   4. Large type books
   I. Title
   823.9′2 [F]

   ISBN 1–84395–698–5

Published by
F. A. Thorpe (Publishing)
Anstey, Leicestershire

Set by Words & Graphics Ltd.
Anstey, Leicestershire
Printed and bound in Great Britain by
T. J. International Ltd., Padstow, Cornwall

This book is printed on acid-free paper

1

Tanwen Jones looked up from studying the map spread out across her steering-wheel, to meet the dark eyes of the man scowling in at her through the half-open window.

'This isn't a public road, you know.'

'I was rapidly coming to that conclusion myself,' she replied with a smile, pushing away a blonde curl that had escaped from its restraining scrunchy, and now half-obscured her heart-shaped face dominated by large hazel eyes. 'I think I must have taken a wrong turning.'

'You should have looked at that before you set out,' he returned, clearly oblivious to this peaceable approach.

'I did.'

Tanni's good humour began to slip.

'It's easy to get confused on these winding roads, and with so many tracks

1

leading off, I can't be the first person to make a mistake.'

The frown did now waver. If anything, his slate-grey eyes watched her with even more suspicion than before. He looked just the sort, Tani thought sourly, to try to terrorise any passing female, and then go home to feed bread and water to his wife locked up in the attic of whatever god-forsaken hovel lurked behind the thick screen of beech trees at the end of the track!

With the latest slanging-match with James still seething in her mind, she was in no mood to have any more dealings than she had to with narrow-minded idiots whose sole aim in life was to keep all and sundry off their land.

It was only sheep fields, for heaven's sake, acres and acres of them, stretching across the undulating hillsides, as far as the eye could see, until they met the steeper slopes of the higher mountains, where the estuary finally petered out into pools and marshland. It was all

2

very picturesque, and she'd been admiring the distant drama of the far peaks all the way since the road had left the coast at the last little seaside town, and followed the estuary inland. It had made her feel that James and his impossible demands were very far away, and left her with a cheerful sense that she was going to enjoy the next three months, whatever he said.

'There's a turning point just over the bridge.'

'Thank you.'

She forced herself to keep as much of an edge out of her voice as possible. She was tired, she was late, and she was lost, and for the past half-hour she had seen nothing but sheep and the occasional herd of cattle, who were not exactly promising when it came to seeking directions.

'I suppose you couldn't tell me where I can find Theodesa Abbey?' she enquired.

The man snorted, with undisguised contempt.

'So you're another one after the Ivory Princess,' he said. 'Getting your kicks from someone else's misfortune, very civilised.'

'Look,' Tani said, patience flying rapidly out of he window, 'I've been hired to do a job, if you don't mind, strictly for the money. No-one has mentioned any princess to me, so I'll decide for myself where I get my kicks, thank you very much.'

There was a moment's silence, while she battled between pride and an urgent desire to wind up the window, lock the doors and make a bolt for it. Perhaps there were advantages to electric windows and central locking, she considered.

The scowl, however, had eased a little, leaving her opponent looking slightly less like a homicidal maniac, not much, but enough for her to feel safe to wait around for his answer. He was, in fact, scrutinising her intently, as if to make certain he would know her again wherever they met. Perhaps it was a secret army base down there, she thought. Her imagination, as James so frequently pointed out, was apt to run away with her.

She could already see satellite dishes, underground bases, and dogs that could have your leg off soon as look at you!

'Next turning on the right.'

'Oh.'

She came crashing back to earth.

'And tell Heston to give his hired help better directions from now on.'

Charming! She should leave it like that, and get out of here. When he was not going on about her over-active imagination, James had taken to informing her that temper of hers would get her into deep trouble one day.

'It might help if you had a sign at the end of the track, if you don't want visitors,' she snapped.

But this time she did have the sense to have the ignition turned, and the car in first gear before she had stopped speaking, and be off like a shot before he could reply.

The turning place over the bridge was tight, to put it mildly, with a ditch ready to catch out the unwary on both sides. Tanwen gritted her teeth, and made the turn as neatly as she could, making sure she went nowhere near the ditches, aware of the owner of the track making his way towards her in a decidedly purposeful way, as if he did not consider her last remarks the end of the matter.

Fortunately, she had completed the turn by the time he reached the bridge, and she sailed by him without even a look in his direction, making her way back towards the road as rapidly as she dared. A glance in her mirror every now and then told her that he was still standing on the bridge, watching her until she had disappeared from sight.

* * *

'So you met the delightful Morris, then.' Alys laughed. 'Don't take any notice of him. He's all talk, as far as I can see.'

She lifted a bag out of the boot of Tanwen's car, and slung it over one shoulder.

'I thought he and poor Heston would have made up their differences years ago, but he always sends the same message.'

'I'm not the only one, then, to make that mistake.'

Tani was relieved. Upsetting the neighbours was not exactly a good start to her new employment.

'Oh, no, not by a long shot. I'm sure at least half my archaeology students ended up being run off his land. I don't know why he doesn't put up a sign. It would save everyone a lot of hassle.'

'That's what I said.'

'You told him that, to his face?'

Alys gazed at her, either in admiration, or with a faint suspicion that she was quite mad. Which, Tani was not entirely sure.

'Well, he was so rude. And anyone

can make mistakes,' she replied.

'And you lived to tell the tale, you see, so he can't be all bad. I've always found him to be OK whenever I've had dealings with him.'

Tani looked at her new acquaintance, and smiled. Somehow, she'd imagined the director of the archaeological dig alongside the abbey to be gravel-voiced and ancient, permanently ingrained with dirt, and with a taste for whisky. The young woman who had come out to greet her at the sound of her approaching car was no older than herself, and very small and neat, with a mass of soft-gold hair twisted up behind her head in an intricate metal clasp, and with an open and trusting expression in her blue eyes, as if she could never bear to think ill of anybody. No-one in their right mind, Tani felt, could possibly be offensive to Alys.

'Come on,' Alys said, as Tani finished locking the car. 'I'll show you to your room.'

'Room? I thought we were all in a barn?'

'Well, the students still are. We're lucky. Some of the conversions that are going to be self-catering accommodation have been finished early. They're a bit basic, but at least we've got a proper bathroom, a kitchen and real beds. Sheets, even.'

'And here am I with my sleeping-bag, all ready to pick straw out of my hair!'

'Me, too. The students think we're mad not to stay in the barn, but I just told them it was so they could party in peace. I couldn't let them think we are wimps, now, could I?'

Tani laughed, and followed her new friend through a large gateway, and inside the high, stone walls. She found herself crossing a courtyard, paved with small, uneven cobbles that looked as if they had been there since at least the Dark Ages. All around rose equally ancient-looking walls, with small, paned windows. Wooden doors, some old and dilapidated, others clearly new, led into interesting-looking spaces, much of it only half-finished. There was accommodation on one side, shops and display rooms on the other. It all looked very empty, as if nothing had been moved in yet.

'This isn't the abbey then?' she asked, doubtfully.

'Oh, no. This is the manor house that was built much later. The abbey is only a ruin, over there, see?'

Tani followed her pointing finger to where empty, stone arches rose, just visible, on higher ground behind the courtyard.

'The abbey was built in the Middle Ages by Prince Estyn, who ruled most of the countryside from here to the sea, and lived in the castle that once stood on that small hill just behind the abbey, the one with all the oaks. You can still make out a couple of the towers amongst the trees.'

Just was the right word — a couple of very tatty-looking piles of stone was all that could be seen. Tani took pride in her job, but if they asked her to create detailed reconstructions of the way the castle might have looked once from that kind of evidence, they'd another think coming. She looked dubiously at Alys, who appeared to have read her thoughts, and was smiling reassuringly.

'We won't have time to do much about the castle this year,' she said. 'And anyhow, it's the abbey that's the real interesting bit. Prince Estyn built it in memory of his wife, Theodesa.'

Tani looked blank.

'You know, the Ivory Princess,' Alys went on.

What was it that Morris had said about an Ivory Princess and getting kicks out of someone else's misfortune?

'I'm sorry,' Tani said, feeling this was another not-very-good start to the summer. 'This was all very last minute. No-one had time to send me any information.'

This was not entirely true. There had been a whole week, in fact, after the panic call to say that the illustrator for a big, new historical project had foolishly gone skiing, and even more foolishly fallen and broken her drawing wrist, and, yes, it was short notice, but could she possibly help out? Could she! With even two broken legs she would — a whole summer of drawing abbeys, castles, knights in armour and mediaeval ladies complete with exotic headdresses — no contest, especially when the other choice was to spend the days cataloguing yet more bones in the museum, and the evenings listening to James deep in the ill-tempered throes of trying to get his latest play on to the laptop.

All the same, an entire week was not impossible for the promised information to have been sent, but Tani had no wish to go into this with her new friend. She was quite certain it was an innocent mistake, and had no desire to embarrass her.

'Really?'

Alys was looking at her in surprise.

'Oh, well, come in here then.'

She pushed open a heavy, wooden door just in front of them, and led Tani into a large, shadowy space, lit only by streams of light beaming down from several skylights in the roof.

'Put your bags down here. They'll be fine.'

Alys felt around for a moment, and found the switch that sent a myriad of small spotlights glowing around the walls, revealing glass display cases of various sizes, and a network of empty information stands.

'This is the museum and information centre for the abbey. It's not nearly finished, of course.'

She turned to Tani and smiled.

'We'll need you to provide the illustrations for the information areas.'

'They're huge!'

Tani wasn't quite sure if she was more nervous or excited. She'd never done anything for such a vast and public space before.

'Most of the display cases are empty, too. Lots of things haven't arrived yet, of course, and the stands over there . . .'

Alys pointed to a particularly dark corner without any lighting.

'Well, those are for the finds we make at the dig.'

The two young women exchanged glances of mutual understanding. Even in the gloom, the cases looked alarmingly large. Filling them sounded an even scarier proposition than providing enough drawings to fill the stands. At least, Tanwen reflected, she would have the information provided for her. Poor Alys would always have the unnerving thought that maybe there was nothing at all to find in her dig.

'I'm sure it will be fine,' she said.

'Me, too. Come on, I want to show you this.'

Alys led the way to the very centre of the museum. There, a large rectangle had been sunk into the tiled floor, and in the middle had been placed a flat piece of marble, of the kind found on old memorial plaques. Swathes of purple rope prevented the watchers from falling into the sunken area, but allowed them to gaze down on the intricate carving.

'It's beautiful.'

Tani gazed entranced at the life-size figure of a woman lying apparently asleep at the centre of the stone. Her long gown flowed as if it were made of silk, with neat little slippers peeping out at the bottom. All around her was woven a pattern of flowers and leaves, with small, stylised animals peering out from the spaces in between.

'We were lucky to get her,' Alys added. 'She was in Llanestyn Heritage Centre, nearly an hour's drive from here, until Easter. They didn't want to let go of her at all. Heston had to fight tooth and nail to get her here. She's the main visitor attraction of the whole area, you see.'

'Oh.'

Tani looked down into the peaceful face, surrounded by long locks of flowing hair. It was a gentle face, she thought, and extraordinarily beautiful, with its aquiline nose and arched eyebrows, and yet, without quite knowing how, it was a face that held an expression of infinite sadness, as if all joy in life had once been snatched from its owner.

'Is that . . . ' she whispered.

'Yes, that's her. That's the Ivory Princess,' Alys said.

2

'She isn't really made of ivory, of course,' Alys said. 'No-one knows quite how she got that name. It's quite a rare stone, only found in a quarry in Cornwall, so one theory is that people in the past believed it was a kind of ivory, or maybe it was just because it was rare, and ivory was also rare. We'll probably never know.'

'The man next door said something about a misfortune. Did she have a really tragic story, then?'

'Oh, very. She was supposed to be the youngest daughter of a Syrian king. The story goes that Prince Estyn arranged to marry her, probably to do with prestige, and trade routes, that kind of thing, because he couldn't ever have met her. Anyhow, he obviously hadn't heard of Tristan and Isolde, because he sent his younger brother to fetch her.'

'Bad move.'

'Well, exactly. So they promptly fell in love on the way back, and when Prince Estyn found out, he is supposed to have gone into such a rage he struck his brother and killed him. He was very sorry afterwards, and made him a very grand funeral casket to show just how sorry he was. He still married the princess, of course.'

'Charming,' Tani said.

'There were some advantages of being a mere peasant in those days,' Alys agreed. 'Anyhow, Theodesa's heart was well and truly broken, and it was said she never smiled again. Every evening at sunset she would visit the casket where her lover was buried, and one morning she was found there, dead.'

'That is so sad,' Tani said.

Morris did have a point, she admitted, grudgingly. What on earth would the Ivory Princess be feeling if she could see them now, preparing to make a visitor attraction out of her sad tale?

'Is that why this carving was made?'

'Sort of. You see, that's not quite the end of the story. Just as Prince Estyn was mourning his wife, there was a huge earthquake that destroyed part of his castle, and completely buried his brother's funeral casket. The landslide is still clearly visible, on the other side of the abbey. We're concentrating the excavations there, in case the story is true and there really is a casket somewhere underneath. Well, of course, Prince Estyn believed the disaster was the lovers getting their own back, so he never repaired the castle, but paid for the building of the abbey instead. Some stories even say he spent the rest of his life as a monk, just to make sure there was no comeback for him in the after-life. Whatever the truth, this stone was found, when they first started excavating the abbey, back in the fifties, and visitors have been flocking here ever since, which was why the Theodesa Trust was set up, to protect and improve the site.'

'And why we've got jobs here,' Tani added, thoughtfully.

'Morris again?'

'Sort of.'

'Don't take any notice. He's always had a soft spot for the princess for some reason. Heston thinks it's to do with even more people to cross his land by mistake in the summer season, but I'm not sure. Anyhow, I'm supposed to be getting you settled in. You'll have plenty time to find out all you want to later. Come on. Heston will be wondering where on earth we have got to.'

Crossing the rest of the courtyard, the two young women stopped at a bright red door, complete with a brass knocker made in the shape of a mediaeval tower. Alys pushed the door open, and they stepped into a small, white-washed corridor, with wooden doors leading off on either side. It smelled strongly of new paint and bleach.

'Come into the kitchen,' Alys said, leading the way.

They stepped into a much lighter room, with a pine table at its centre, and a staircase leading off to the rest of the house. Beyond it lay a small, but neatly-fitted kitchen, with a large french window that led into a garden beyond.

'There you are. We were beginning to think you'd managed to get lost.'

A woman rose from a chair on the small patio outside the french windows, and came in to greet them. She was a few years older than Alys, tall, with long black hair hanging loose down her back, and eyes of a particularly intense blue-green. Her trouser-suit was neatly fitted, showing an elegant figure to its best advantage.

Tani immediately became aware that her own hair was decidedly dishevelled from being blown about by the rush of air coming through her open car window, and that her trousers were of the comfortable and baggy variety, and very creased.

'Sorry, Kirstin,' Alys said quickly. 'It was my fault. I stopped to show Tanwen the museum on the way. She hadn't had much information, so I thought . . . '

Her voice trailed off, apologetically, and, for a moment, she looked more like a child than ever.

'Really.' There was a faintly disapproving edge to Kirstin's voice, but she added pleasantly enough, 'Well, we are all glad that you could make it, Tanwen,' as a tall figure appeared from the garden. 'Aren't we, Heston?'

'Don't know what we would have done without you,' the new arrival said in cheerful tones. 'Historical illustrators are a rare breed, you know, especially at short notice.'

'You're making me nervous,' Tani confessed, with a smile. 'You haven't even seen my work yet.'

'Ah, but we have our spies,' Heston replied.

The moment he stepped inside, the kitchen appeared even smaller than before. He was tall, and strongly-built, with long, narrow hands, that had the look of being capable both of finesse and strength. His hair was a pale gold, almost bleached to white by the sun, and his light blue eyes were currently watching Tani's sudden look of alarm with a touch of amusement.

'Don't worry,' he added. 'I happened to be in London a few months ago. Your museum was one of the places I visited. I remembered being impressed by the illustrations, so when Mari opted to take a running jump at a tree like that, I remembered them. I'm just glad we managed to prise you away for the summer,' he added with a smile.

'Mari didn't intend to break her wrist,' Alys protested.

'Heston was only joking,' Kirstin said, a little severely, rather than as if she did indeed see the archaeologist as no older than a child. 'I'm sure he didn't mean it.'

'No, of course not,' Heston said, good-humouredly. 'You should know me by now, Alys.'

'Yes, yes, of course.'

A faint suspicion of a blush crept

over Alys's pretty features, causing Kirstin to eye her with a slight frown. Tani noted to herself, better to stay well clear of this one. So much for James bemoaning the fact that she was bound to fall promptly in love with the director of the Theodesa Trust, and he would never see her again. At the time, Tani remembered, with an inward cringe, she had been in such a fury she had yelled back in no uncertain terms that it wouldn't need any director, no matter how handsome, to have that effect, and she'd start packing now, if that's what James wanted.

She'd have done it, too, except that when he had calmed down, James had been very sweet, and very apologetic, and she'd come back from work that night to find her favourite meal cooked, and a bottle of wine. After the second glass, they had both been contrite, and promised each other to work hard to sort it all out, and make it just as it had been, right in the beginning. She'd even secretly considered turning down the job at the Trust, but then their promises had begun to fall apart again before the next day was out, and she'd known that what she needed — what they both needed — right at this moment, was time and space to work out what they really wanted.

She looked up to find Heston watching her face, in a thoughtful manner.

'I met your neighbour,' she said abruptly, with a sudden desire to hide any of her thoughts which might have crept into her face.

'Did you?'

Heston frowned, and a chill glint came into his eyes.

'I hope he didn't prove too offensive.'

'No, not very,' she said. 'I was driving down his track, even though it was a mistake.'

'So he's still not put that sign up.' Kirstin frowned. 'We can't have that, you know, Heston, when we start having visitors arriving. I'll have another word with him in the morning.'

'No, it's all right.' Heston sighed, but the smile was back on his face. 'I'll go and speak to him. He must be as sick of this situation as we are. I'm sure he'll see sense in the end.'

'Ha!'

Kirstin, it seemed, had no time whatsoever for the irascible Morris. Undisguised contempt laced her exclamation. Heston, however, ignored her doubts, and smiled again at Tani.

'I'm glad you made it, anyhow, Tanwen, troublesome neighbours and all. I hope you settle in all right. Everything should be here, but if you need anything, please come over and let me or Kirstin know. We're in the offices next door to the museum.'

'Thank you,' Tani replied.

He vanished, and the kitchen seemed to resume its former size. Kirstin, however, lingered a moment or two longer.

'He didn't actually threaten you, did he?' she asked.

'Morris? No. He seemed angry, but that was all.'

Kirstin seemed a little disappointed.

'Well, I'd just keep as far away from him as possible in future. Morris, I'm afraid, is nothing but trouble.'

'He's never actually harmed anyone,' Alys exclaimed.

'Not physically, no, but there are other ways, you know.'

Alys subsided, a look of awkwardness on her face, as if suddenly coming up against an unpleasant fact she had been attempting to avoid.

'And anyhow, we don't know what he might have done, had he not been stopped in time.'

Kirstin met Tanwen's eyes.

'Apart from what he did to Heston,' she said, firmly. 'There was a small matter of handling stolen goods, and fraud. He can count himself lucky he wasn't locked away for a very long time, if you ask me. Like I said, the farther you stay away from him the better.'

There was a moment's silence.

'I'll show you to your room,' Alys said, at last.

'And I'd better get on,' Kirstin said. 'There's so much to do if we are to open at the beginning of August. I'm glad you arrived safely, Tanwen, and I look forward to working with you.'

'Me, too,' Tani replied, although privately she wasn't sure.

Kirstin seemed quite high-powered and efficient, and not one to suffer fools gladly. Tani had a nasty feeling she might find herself inhabiting the last category before long.

'What does Kirstin actually do?' she enquired, as she followed Alys up the stairs.

'She's the Project Manager, who mostly looks after the setting up of the museum,' Alys replied. 'She's also the Director of the Heritage Centre in Llanestyn, so Heston is very lucky to have her.'

She turned round and smiled.

'She's a bit overpowering at first, but she's OK after a bit.'

At the top of the stairs there was a small landing. All the doors were wide open, revealing a bathroom, and three bedrooms.

'We've put you in this one, next to mine,' Alys said, 'overlooking the courtyard.'

She indicated the door opposite.

'That one is bigger, and has a much better view, right over the grounds. But Kirstin is using that one for when she and Heston are working late. She's got a house just outside Llanestyn, but it's a long drive back, especially at night.'

Alys seemed to feel this called for further explanation.

'And it's often nice to relax with a drink after work and talk things through. It's really quite a tight schedule, you see.'

'I understand,' Tani replied.

It was a pity about the view, she thought, seeing a glimpse of a ruined arch, and rolling fields beyond through the window of Kirstin's room. Her own was quite small, with two single beds, and, as Alys had said, a view that took in only the cobbles and the surrounding buildings of the courtyard. But still, this was luxury after the accommodation she had been expecting. There was a pine wardrobe, and one of the beds had been freshly made up, while a small bunch of highly-scented freesias was placed in front of the mirror on a small dressing-table next to the window, helping to dispel the all-pervasive smell of paint.

'I do hope it's all right,' Alys said.

'It's lovely,' Tani replied.

'Oh, good. This is mine, they're all much the same.'

Alys led her into a slightly smaller room with bunk beds, clearly aimed at the children of the family.

'Alys, are you sure — '

'Of course, I am. I've always wanted to sleep on the top of a bunk bed, ever since I was little. My sister always hogged the top. She was older, and bigger. We're the same size now, of course, when it's too late.'

Tani laughed, but all the same she still felt it was rather unfair that Kirstin, who was only going to sleep there occasionally, had somehow landed herself with the best room. Still, there was nothing she could do about it, she considered, ruefully. She was supposed to be doing this to get away from arguments, and here she was having launched herself into one serious row already.

The memory of her confrontation on the track brought another question back into her mind. She took a quick look at Alys, and then began, hesitantly.

'That thing that Kirstin said about Morris, not that thing about fraud, and that — '

'You mean the part about him harming Heston?'

'Yes.'

She saw Alys sigh, and turn to look out of the window.

'It's not a secret. Everybody still talks about it. It was about three years ago, just before I came. Heston and Morris had been friends for years, you know,' she added looking round. 'But then

31

Heston found out that Morris had been having an affair with his wife.'

'Oh.'

Tani looked at her in surprise. No-one had mentioned about Heston having a wife. That would have shut James up a bit, or perhaps not, under the circumstances.

'Such a pity. She's apparently a really nice woman. Not the kind you think of doing anything like that, not with your husband's best friend, anyhow.'

She'd be a fool to exchange a man like Heston for such an ill-tempered petty criminal, Tani added to herself.

'So what happened?'

'Well, according to people in the village, when Heston found out what had been going on, Suzie ran off in the middle of the night and went to live with Morris.'

'Never!'

Tani looked at her in astonishment. The thought of any woman living with her enemy of the track was quite beyond her, and right next door to your ex-husband, rubbing his nose in it, so to speak.

'She's still there, they say, living in that old cottage of his. Mind you, no-one has seen her for years.'

A small shiver went down Tani's back.

'Hasn't anyone tried to visit her, even?'

'I suppose so. I think Heston went once or twice. Kirstin always said he came back in a really foul mood, and wouldn't speak to anyone, which is not like Heston at all. So I suppose he didn't even get to see her. I'm sure she's fine. Doesn't want to meet all the gossip, I expect. You know what places like these are like.'

'I suppose so.'

All the same, Tani frowned and changed the subject. It seemed even more of a pity about Kirstin's room, she reflected. She was sure she had caught a glimpse of a house in the distance, in the direction where Morris's land lay. Maybe it was even possible to see if there was a light on there at night, not that that would tell you much, of course, but it might be a start.

Well, well, well, Tani thought to herself, and there she was, thinking it was only a several-hundred-year-old mystery she was here to uncover. Whatever happened, she was not about to miss this for the world.

3

Tani had gone to bed so tired that she was convinced that she could sleep for at least a week. All the same, it was the quiet of early morning when she awoke to the soft light creeping in between the flowered curtains, and the chatter of birds amongst the courtyard roofs. She was still tired, she could feel it, but it was quite impossible to turn over and go to sleep again. She got up, and went to look out of the window.

Below her, the courtyard was deserted. She could just make out the outline of the ruined abbey in the distance, mist still clinging to the arches as it drifted away slowly to reveal the blue of a perfect summer sky. Already, Tani mused to herself, she felt different, almost as if a large weight had been lifted from her shoulders, and left her with the curiosity and the energy she had known as a child, and had recently been convinced she would never feel again.

Suddenly light-hearted, she was determined to make the most of this precious moment of solitude before the working day began. She slipped into a pair of jeans, and pulled her favourite over-sized jumper over her pyjama top. Her mass of fair hair always took some time to coax into any semblance of order, and so she opted not to even try. The only people she was likely to meet, she reasoned, were the students camped in the barn, and, from her brief introduction to them last night, scrubbed cleanliness and neatness were the last things on their mind.

She shoved all the recalcitrant hair she could find into an ancient scrunchy she always kept at hand to keep stray hairs from marring her water-colour sketches before they were dry. Then she slipped downstairs as quietly as she could, and into the kitchen.

Outside, in the little garden, the air was fresh. At the end of the garden there was a small, wooden gate set into the ivy of the stone walls. Tani had noticed it last night, and now hoped it was not the kind of gate that was kept locked, as it offered the most direct route towards the distant arches. It opened easily, without even a creak to betray her, and she found herself in a wide stretch of open field, with the stone arches towering above her.

'Wow,' Tani whispered to herself, watching the mist roll across the grass and curve around the delicately-carved ruins of the old abbey.

She walked down the wide aisle between the remaining columns, imagining so easily the glory of its past — the huge arch of the roof, the glow of the stories portrayed in the stained glass of the windows, and the calm and the quiet of lives lived in contemplation.

'This is not a nunnery, you know.'

Tani whirled around at the voice behind her, shattering her peace.

'I beg your pardon.'

For one horrible moment, she was

convinced the dark hair of the man stepping out from between the columns was that of the dreaded Morris, and that somehow she had strayed on to his land once more, and yesterday's nightmare was about to begin all over again. But, as he drew closer, she could see he was taller, and of a stronger build, the curl of his hair long enough to reach his shoulders, while the smile on his wide mouth was unlike any she could ever expect to see on the face of yesterday's opponent.

The dark eyes were watching her with amusement rather than hostility, and with an open admiration that made her glad of her enveloping jumper.

'Why should it be a nunnery?' she returned, frowning a little, poised between dignity and an awareness that she was out of shouting distance of the buildings, and that she had not so much as a mobile phone with her.

'Standing there, you looked like a nun, deep in contemplation,' he replied, with a smile.

Tani's frown deepened. She had a feeling she was being gently teased, and she could feel her dignity slipping.

'I'm no nun,' she retorted, reflecting a little too late that, under the circumstances, this might not be the wisest of things to say.

Sure enough, the smile widened even further.

'I'm glad to hear it.'

'I didn't mean — '

'I'm sure you didn't, which, in one way, is a pity. But, on the other hand, I wouldn't like anything to come in the way of the enjoyment of the chase.'

Tani found herself glaring at him, every insult she'd ever wanted to say to sleaze-bags eyeing her up rushing headlong to her lips. At the last moment, she caught the look in his eyes, and stopped.

'You're winding me up,' she said.

She was rewarded by a heartly laugh, accompanied by a mischievous twinkle in his deep blue eyes.

'Rumbled again,' he remarked with a

39

grin. 'And there you are, looking even prettier when you are angry.'

'Oh, please,' Tani returned, tartly, 'you might at least be original.'

The laugh came again. It was an infectious laugh, that had Tani's lips twitching despite herself. Outrageous comments or not, she no longer felt any kind of threat in his presence, and there was an easy charm to his manner that made her feel that she had known him all her life. In fact, come to think of it, there was something familiar in his face.

She took a swift look at the strong features, with the chiselled nose, and the firm line of his jaw, even more certain she had met him before, although where, she could not for the life of her remember.

'I'm Tanwen Jones,' she said, abruptly.

'Ah, the illustrator.'

To her relief, his tone was simply that of curiosity satisfied.

'Heston's saviour.'

'Hardly.'

'You didn't see the panic when Mari's mother phoned with the bad news. Heston lives for his work, you know, and you could see the abyss of failure opening up before him. Pictures always speak louder than words, and a display without illustrations would have had visitors running for the hills, which would not have looked good.'

'I suppose not.'

'You'll have your work cut out,' he remarked.

'I can see.'

He was behaving, Tani thought with some irritation, as if she should know exactly who he was, and had no need to introduce himself at all. Was it a touch of arrogance she detected at the corners of his smile? He probably believed himself so important that she knew who he was by instinct, she added, her recent sour mood in danger of returning. Well, he could be royalty, as far as she cared. She had come here to get away from the unpredictable moods of one man, and she had no intention of

41

throwing herself into the path of another, however attractive. She opted to go into business mode, and keep the whole thing firmly impersonal.

'It's much larger than I thought it would be. I can only see it in bits from here. It really needs a view from farther away to get an idea of the whole picture within the landscape. You don't know if it's possible to get into those fields.'

She waved towards the sheep fields below the hill.

'That would be ideal.'

Her companion grunted ruefully.

'Not unless you want to brave man-traps and Rottweilers,' he answered dryly. 'The owner is not exactly co-operative in such things.'

'Oh.'

There was no doubt in Tani's mind as to who that owner could be. Was the abbey completely surrounded by Morris's land? This could begin to feel like a siege.

'It's worth a try, though.'

He smiled at her, eyes lingering over

the escaping tendrils of hair settling one by one around her face.

'Kirstin is the one to approach him. She's negotiated access to the hill, to save us taking equipment all the way around to where the Trust part starts. I'm sure she can persuade Morris to allow us to use part of his land. I need to see Kirstin this morning. I'll ask her, if you like.'

'That's not necessary,' she replied.

She couldn't have him thinking she could not fight her own battles.

'Oh, not at all. It's no trouble. We'll need to go over there to get some shots for the cameras anyhow.' He grinned. 'Which will at least ensure the dogs and the guns stay out of our way. Morris never could bear to see himself on TV.'

'Oh,' Tani said.

She swallowed hard, and tried her very best not to let her mouth fall right open. Of course! Just how stupid could she be? No wonder he hadn't introduced himself. There wasn't a red-blooded female in the western world, and no doubt far beyond, who wouldn't know who he was. Admittedly he had been out of the tabloids, and off the prime-time screens for a while, working on some new project, but still she should have known.

'Thank you,' she muttered lamely.

'Any time.'

His grin was slightly rueful, as if he had suddenly discovered he had broken a spell, and the story was about to turn rather unpleasant. Her younger sister, Cadi, would no doubt have been gibbering by now, but Tani wasn't some silly idiot about to fall at his feet.

'So, I take it you're filming the restoration of the abbey?' she said casually.

'That's the idea.'

He gave her a quick glance, as if grateful she was continuing the conversation as normal, and not falling about screaming, and trying to tear strips off his jacket.

'I've known Heston for years. We were at college together, in fact. He seemed so excited about this Ivory Princess, it seemed too good a chance to miss. It took a bit of negotiation in the right quarters, but I managed to persuade them.'

She bet he could. Tani knew very little about the media world, but she was quite certain no-one would be able to resist Lyndon Hawksmoor when he put his mind to it. Just voted most gorgeous man on the planet for the third year running, he was reportedly the single-handed reason for the sudden upshot of interest in mediaeval history at schools and universities. Tani herself had followed, entranced, his various television series on the lives of kings, as he strode about the countryside in full costume recreating battles and power-struggles, passionate love affairs and betrayals, with such enthusiasm.

One or two of her stuffier colleagues at the museum had scoffed at this pollution of historical fact, but there was no denying his popularity. Every school party that came into the museum was full of him. The boys adored the sword rattling, while the girls simply adored him. If there was ever a man you wanted to step out from the dawn mist, and turn those dark eyes in your direction . . . Tani quickly thrust such thoughts from her mind.

'Sounds like good publicity for the abbey,' she said.

'I hope so. There is never enough money for projects like these, so hopefully this will help.'

'Heston must be pleased.'

'It could make his life easier, I suppose, with the publicity.'

The smile appeared in her direction again.

'Although, knowing Heston, I'm sure he'd be happy going on with no interference at all.'

Tani returned his smile, still attempting to reconcile the romantic figure of the television screen with the quietly-charming man beside her who had made no attempt to impress her with mention of his fame.

'I'd better go,' she said, just a little reluctantly. 'I didn't tell anyone where I was going. They'll be wondering where I am.'

'I'll come with you then, if I may. I'm supposed to be meeting Heston for breakfast. It's the only time he has free at the moment,' he added at her look of surprise at this rather unorthodox arrangement, 'which suits me. I'm a great one for atmospheric shots at dawn. In fact, I'd have hauled the camera crew along if I'd have realised it was going to be such a perfect morning.'

Mischief appeared in those eyes again.

'Then you'd have found yourself playing a nun for real. It looked so perfect, no-one would have let you say no.'

'Then I'm glad you didn't,' Tani returned. 'The last time I wanted to be a film star was when I was still dressing up in my mother's wedding dress, just after the ballerina phase.'

Lyndon laughed.

'You've not escaped yet, you know. This looks just the right place for a few ghosts.'

'In your dreams.'

Tani smiled as they began to walk back towards the walls of the manor house, just as the sun broke through the mist.

'Thanks,' Lyndon muttered, suddenly serious.

'I didn't do anything,' Tani said, turning towards him in some surprise.

'Exactly. Look. I know I'm lucky, and I have a job to die for, but that is all it is, a job. That isn't really me on the screen, just a rôle I play, almost like an actor, if you see what I mean. Most people confuse the two, and, well, it gets a bit over the top.'

'That's OK,' Tani said, a little awkwardly.

This wasn't exactly her everyday kind of conversation, and she wasn't quite sure how to react.

'You treated me, well, just as me. I

appreciate that.'

A brief shadow passed across his features.

'It isn't always how it seems. There are things — expectations — '

He paused, and looked earnestly into her face.

'Look, Tanwen, it isn't always easy to speak to the people around me, and everyone else they keep away. I just — I just need — '

He stopped abruptly, and drew away from her.

'I agree, that will certainly be the best location,' he said loudly, in the tones of one continuing a conversation.

'A bit of an early start, isn't it?'

Tani turned to discover Kirstin standing by the main gate to the courtyard, watching them both with narrowed eyes.

'Best time to catch the atmosphere of the place,' Lyndon replied, turning towards Tani, a silent pleading in his eyes. 'Don't you think so, Tanwen?'

'Oh, yes,' she said. 'You really get a

flavour of how it must have been.'

He flashed a brief smile of unmistakable gratitude in her direction, before stepping forward to slip his arm through that of Kirstin in a playfully flirtatious manner.

'Gorgeous as ever, Kirstin, my dear. You break every heart that comes in your direction.'

'Don't be ridiculous,' she replied, but Tani could hear the triumphant purr in her voice, as the two walked on ahead, Lyndon continuing his flattery in an over-cheerful manner.

Tani followed them in silence. Lyndon neither spoke to her, nor looked in her direction, but there was something in his tone that made her certain he was aware of her every step. Whatever he had been about to say troubled him, and he clearly had no wish for it to be public knowledge, and, by his own account, he had few, if any, he could confide in. Both working here for the next few weeks at least, there were bound to be times when they would meet again, and maybe

without anyone to overhear their conversation.

This, Tani was quite certain, was not
the end of the matter.

4

The next few weeks passed in a daze. Tani was so busy she had little time to ponder on the strange events on that first morning, or to wonder what it might have been that Lyndon had been trying to confide in her. This was just as well, as there had certainly been no time for the two of them to speak alone. In fact, Tani reflected, it almost seemed at times as if Lyndon was deliberately avoiding her.

He was friendly enough when they passed during the course of the day, or found themselves next to each other in the queue at the canteen, but he showed no desire to sit and talk to her, particularly, she couldn't help noticing, when Kirstin was around.

'Has Kirstin known him long?' she asked Alys one day, as they sat at lunch with the students.

'Who, Lyndon?'

'Yes.'

'Not especially. Kirstin was one of the historical advisors on his last series, but he hasn't mentioned working with her before that. Why?'

'Oh, no reason.'

'If you think she looks as if she fancies him madly, well, she does,' Alys said with a smile, 'but that's nothing new, and I expect he's used to it. I'm sure it's water off a duck's back to him.'

'That sounds very cynical,' Tani said, surprised by the unexpected sharpness in her friend's tone.

'Does it? I suppose I'm just not into flashy media types, or those who suck up to them,' she added, glancing to where Kirstin was sitting across from Lyndon, playing with a collection of salad leaves on her plate, and clearly hanging on to his every word.

Alys, Tani reflected, had every reason to dislike Kirstin. That brief exchange of glances over Heston on her first night had given her reason enough for the two women's coolness towards each other. In that case, Alys should be pleased that Kirstin appeared to have transferred her ambitions so swiftly and completely, unless she was playing some double game that still kept Heston hanging on, of course. Tani frowned at herself for such uncharitable thoughts. She couldn't possibly know how Kirstin behaved in the office when she and Heston were working, and it was none of her business.

And yet, there was something she couldn't quite bring herself to like about Kirstin, nothing she could quite put her finger on, and nothing she had the remotest wish to discuss even with Alys. Kirstin was elegant, beautiful and successful. The fact that the two most eligible bachelors in the place couldn't keep their eyes off her might make any criticism from Tani seem like feminine jealousy, and maybe that was all it was. She had to consider the fact. Lyndon had been more than happy to give his whole attention to her until Kirstin came on the scene.

Tani watched the two closely as they finished their lunch and began to make their way towards the students' table on their way out. Lyndon had behaved as if he had not wanted Kirstin to overhear what he had been about to say, or to suspect he had been about to speak of anything out of the ordinary at all, almost, Tani thought, puzzling over the sudden insight, almost as if he were afraid of her.

'Ah, Tani, I wanted to have a quick word.'

Kirstin paused as she passed them.

'Yes?'

'Just to let you know, I've had a word with Morris. He's agreed to allow you and the camera teams on to the field beside the abbey.'

'That's wonderful! Thank you, Kirstin.'

The manager's neatly-clad shoulders shrugged.

'Morris is no problem if you approach him in the right way,' she replied.

As if, Tani thought, everyone else

always goes at it like a bull at a gate. But she contained herself, and merely smiled.

'He's agreed to take the padlock and chain off from tomorrow. Of course, he'll expect no disturbance of the sheep, and any litter to be brought back with you.'

'Of course,' Tani said, ignoring Alys who was going pink beside her with indignation at her friend being spoken to as if she were some species of naughty schoolgirl.

'See you there, then, Tani,' Lyndon called cheerfully, almost as if to make up for his companion's rudeness.

Beside them, Tani was aware, the students were all now hanging eagerly on every word.

'See you,' she muttered, glad to see Kirstin moving on, Lyndon following.

'Did you see that?' the blonde girl beside her was whispering in awe. 'Isn't he just gorgeous? You are so lucky, Tani. Bet we don't get to work with him at all.'

'Oh, I don't know,' Tani said, her sense of humour bubbling up irresistibly at the rather abashed looks on the faces of the boys around her. 'He doesn't ever work up enough sweat to take his shirt off, you know. Talking to cameras is not like a bit of digging. I'll always swop places with you, if you like.'

A burst of laughter went around the table, followed by an eruption of banter on the comparative merits of the various male torsos available for this exchange.

'Tani! You can be quite wicked, on the quiet.'

Alys laughed, as both moved to take their coffee into the comparative quiet of the garden.

'I'm not really,' Tani replied, 'not usually.'

Or, at least, not for a long time. The quick thought came unbidden into her mind, disturbing her with its abruptness. She pushed it away firmly, with an instinct that if she dwelt on it too long she might find herself faced with things she had no wish to face at this moment, and that she might well end up in tears.

'Come on,' she said, 'we've got half an hour left, and I'm determined to make the most of it.'

But the unwelcome thoughts could not be pushed out of Tani's mind for ever.

This came forcibly to Tani a few days later as she sat alone in the field, her easel before her, finishing the last of her watercolour sketches in the warm afternoon light.

She had been absorbed in her task all day, working from the drawings of possible reconstructions of the abbey which Heston had given to her that morning. This was the part of her work she liked best, trying to mould the existing structures into the building they had once been, and attempting to fit it all into the landscape.

Later, back in the small room she had been given as a studio, she would use this to decide on the best scene to bring the ancient world back to life in her finished painting. She made a last sweep of colour, the nearest match to the bloom of heather on the hillside just below the trees, and took the drying picture from the easel to look at it more carefully.

It was all she could do for now. She had all the information she needed to start work on the main picture to greet visitors as they came into the little museum in the courtyard, and give them a flavour of how the abbey might have seemed to all who lived and worked within its walls. Tani laid the picture on her lap, pleased with the day's work.

It was growing late, she suddenly noticed. The sun was almost below the tree line, and a swarm of midges hovered around the edges of the small pool nearby, which had been carved out in a bend in the river. Her stomach grumbled in loud protest at missing lunch as the smell of cooking drifted towards her. An apple and her bottle of mineral water had not quite the same effect as the delicious and substantial meals needed to satisfy the digging and earth-moving activities of the ever-ravenous students.

If she was going to be too busy to be bothered going back to the courtyard to join them, she was definitely bringing sandwiches in future, she told herself, with a smile. Despite the grumbling of her stomach, she remained there, feeling far too contented and relaxed to move.

I haven't felt like this for ages, she thought to herself, and, suddenly, the thought of leaving this peace and going back to Hampstead was utterly unbearable. Of course she'd known it. She'd known it for weeks, months, in fact. Maybe, in his heart of hearts, James knew it, too.

When they were together in the flat and their familiar haunts, with all those dreams and memories between them, it had been impossible to face the truth. But now that she was far away, in utterly new surroundings, the reality was clear. They had found so little to say to each other during their brief phone calls. Even their nightly text messages had become forced, not like the playful exchanges they had once sent to each other.

Tani bent over her picture, a terrible feeling of emptiness inside her. All of a sudden it was quite clear to her that she could not go on like this much longer. She needed to work this out with James, one way or the other, as soon as she was able. Weekends were her own, and she was certain Heston would not object to her going home for a few days, and would not ask any awkward questions.

Unless I sort this out now, she thought to herself, I'll never do it.

However painful it was going to be, it would be far better to split with James now, when there was still a chance they could remain friends, rather than later, when they could well have grown to loathe each other. A tear splashed on to the watercolours of her sketch, scattering the blue of the sky and leaving an uneven blob of white on the paper, but she scarcely noticed.

'You OK?'

The question was abrupt, but not unsympathetic. Tani jumped at this unexpected intrusion into her grief, sending the painting on her lap flying to the ground.

'Fine,' she muttered, hastily dabbing at her eyes with a somewhat grubby sleeve.

A paper handkerchief, thankfully clean, was placed silently into her lap. Tani took it gratefully, glad of the lack of any further questioning. In her present state, she had a nasty feeling she was liable to howl disgracefully on any shoulder offered to her, which was not exactly anything you could easily recover from. There was a short silence, on her companion's part, at least.

Tani, finding herself with nothing to lose, sniffed and blew her nose without any attempt at being discreet about it. When she was finally able to look up without the world swimming around her, she found Morris a short distance from her, painting in one hand, gazing tactfully into the far distance.

'Thanks.'

'That's OK.'

He turned at her words to eye her thoughtfully. Tani swallowed. This was even worse than she had thought, being found sobbing away like some disappointed schoolgirl. The man before her was viewing her with the slate-grey eyes she had last seen glaring at her as she sailed past him on the track. Great! He'd have the shotgun out before she could know it, and she could hardly start to look confident and dignified now.

'I was just going. Kirstin didn't say there was a time limit on being here.'

'There isn't.'

'Don't you want to lock the gate, keep all trespassers out?'

'Not particularly,' Morris replied. 'Not unless you insist, that is.'

'Of course I'm not insisting,' she began crossly.

Those grey eyes were watching her coolly, in a way she was not sure she liked.

'You must be the illustrator.'

'Yes.'

He looked down at her sketch for a few moments.

'Well, they're better than your navigational skills,' he remarked.

Tani glared as, abruptly, a hand was held out towards her.

'Morris.'

There seemed very little choice but to shake it, as briefly as possible, of course.

'Tanwen. Tani.'

'Pleased to meet you, Tani,' he said, wryly, and Tani found herself blushing furiously with embarrassment.

Her little victory of the other day had been well and truly blown out of the water.

'Me, too,' she muttered as she began to gather together her belongings.

'You sure you're OK?'

'Yes, fine. It was nothing, just — '

'All men are brutes?' he suggested, lightly.

Despite herself, Tani laughed, tears welling up in her eyes again.

'Sorry. Didn't mean to pry.'

Tani looked at him in surprise. There was definite sympathy in his voice, and in his eyes, the sort of quiet sympathy that promised endless understanding, and could have you pouring out your troubles in no time. Was that, she wondered, how Suzie had started falling for him, falling for that understanding look, until she found herself in no end of trouble. Considering the general lack of finesse to his manner, it must have been something powerful to make her run away from Heston to be with him. Tani frowned.

'I should hope so,' she said severely.

She expected him to at least return the glare, or walk away at her rudeness, but instead he gave her a rather rueful smile.

'It's just — well — I know what it's like to do something you can spend a lifetime regretting.'

She had to admit it, he had her intrigued. How on earth could anyone be such a mass of contradictions, without any hint of whether he was leaning to the side of the angels or was a perfect monster? And where, she asked herself sharply, bringing herself back to reality with a jolt, just where might Suzie be at this very moment?

'You're wanted,' he said suddenly interrupting her thoughts.

'Sorry?'

'Over there.'

Morris nodded his head briefly towards the manor house, from where the figure of Heston was making his way towards them. She expected him to shoot off into the trees, but he remained, helping her to finish packing away.

'Tani, I thought you might still be here,' Heston said when he reached them, decidedly breathless. 'Alys has been looking for you. She was sure you would want to — '

He stopped abruptly as his eyes fell on her companion. If there had been swords, they might have tried to cut each other to pieces in a moment. As it was, the two men eyed each other in a distinctly frosty silence. It was Morris who broke the awkward pause.

'Heston.'

At least it was a kind of greeting, and better than nothing.

'Morris,' the reply came then silence returned.

'It's all right,' Morris said at last. 'I just came to see how you were all getting on. I'm not about to roar at anyone.'

Heston frowned in reply, and then turned back to Tani.

'Alys was trying to phone you, Tani.'

'Sorry, my mobile battery ran out a couple of hours ago.'

For a moment, she was certain his blue eyes were watching her with suspicion, as if convinced she was lying, and had been up to no good. Was Morris's reputation really that bad?

Mind you, if you were confronted with the man who'd run off with your wife, you were bound to think the worst.

'Oh, well, it's not too late.'

'Too late?'

'They've found something in the trench nearest the hillside, where the deepest part of the landslip was found.'

Morris and his misdemeanours were forgotten, and Heston's eyes were gleaming in undisguised excitement.

'It looks like a stone burial casket, possibly from the same time as that of the Ivory Princess. Alys is hopeful it is still intact. We need to hurry as they're starting to uncover it now.'

'I'll come straight away,' Tani said, slinging her folder and easel over one shoulder, and preparing to follow him.

To her surprise, he didn't rush off. Instead, he paused, and cleared his throat loudly, as if preparing to do something he found less than easy.

'It's not private. You're welcome to join us, if you like, Morris.'

Tani felt her jaw dropping. All right,

she was never going to make this one out. She was even more certain of this when Morris instantly strode towards them with every appearance of eagerness.

'You bet,' he said.

When they arrived at the dig, they found a large crowd gathered around the deep trench. A few curious glances were thrown their way, but the prospect of a major archaeological find clearly outweighed the sight of Morris appearing in their midst.

'Well?' Heston demanded.

'I'm not sure.'

Alys was clambering out, somehow still managing to look remarkably pretty, despite being almost completely covered in earth and mud.

'You must have some idea,' Kirstin said, standing next to Lyndon and the film crew, watching the grubbiness of the proceedings in a rather disdainful manner.

'It could be from the same time, I'm just not certain. I'd prefer a second opinion.'

Tani grinned to herself, as all eyes seemed to be directed instinctively towards Lyndon, who held his hands up, as if to ward off their expectation.

'Hey, don't look at me,' he said. 'I'm no expert.'

'I'd prefer a second opinion,' Alys repeated stubbornly.

There was a moment's silence, a very meaningful silence, Tani suddenly realised, as beside her, Heston began to clear his throat slowly. But, before he could speak, Morris had swung himself down into the trench, and was closely inspecting the corner of carved stone emerging from the surrounding earth.

'D'you have a light?' he called.

'Here, Morris.'

Alys handed down a powerful-looking torch, and rejoined Tani at the edge of the trench.

'Morris will know,' she said.

Kirstin was clearly furious at this turn of events.

'Heston!'

She reached him with a positive hiss in her voice.

'Heston, I am not sure this is at all appropriate. If it is the casket, it clearly can't be moved for some time, and this is not an area that can be easily secured.'

'Nothing is going to happen to the casket.'

Heston was surprisingly firm.

'And it is utterly unfair to put all the responsibility on Alys, when we have an authority on the subject standing by.'

'Didn't you know?' Alys whispered, seeing Tani's enquiring look. 'Morris is the real expert. He was supposed to be the best Professor of Archaeology the university ever had, and he was the director of the Heritage Centre in Llanestyn before Kirstin took over, before all that funny business with the accounts, and things disappearing, and I'm sure that was all a mistake anyhow.'

Beside them, Kirstin was clearly getting nowhere.

'Well, I want it noted that I am not happy about this in the least,' she was saying. 'You'll have that in writing, Heston, first thing tomorrow.'

5

Tani stepped out of the car, stretched her aching back, and sighed. It was so good to be back. It felt like a lifetime since she had left the abbey ground late on Friday afternoon, but now she was back, it almost felt like coming home.

The weekend in London had been difficult. Strangely, James had been almost relieved once she'd told him her reasons for her sudden reappearance, and they had begun talking. It was almost as if he had known the doubts had been hanging over them for a long time. It had all been agreed in a reasonably civilised manner, but that had not made it any easier, packing away the remains of her life at the flat.

At least, as her mother had said, they were only renting, while they had been saving up and looking around for a place of their own to move into when they were married. Just a few months down the line, and things could have been a lot more complicated.

Tani pulled her bag from the boot of the car, and made her way inside the courtyard. Her most precious belongings had been stored back in the spare room at her mum's house, with James having promised to bring the rest round a few days later. Once the work at the abbey was over, she'd have to face the whole business of finding a place to live and maybe a new job.

For all their parting had been fairly amicable, she did not like the thought of bumping into James and his friends on her way to work, or in the local parks and restaurants. It felt, she thought, like the beginning of an entirely new life, and, at the moment, she wasn't sure she had the energy to deal with it all.

The little house was deserted. When she made her way over to the dig, a little while later, she found the students scraping at the earth in a leisurely manner, with no sign of Alys at all.

'She's gone to pick up some archaeological records in Llanestyn,' Heston said with a smile when Tani knocked tentatively on the office door.

'She'll be back just after lunch,' Kirstin added, looking up from her computer screen. 'Was it anything urgent?'

'Oh, no, I just wondered,' Tani said, hastily.

She had no wish to confess that Alys was the only person in whom she had confided her troubles.

'It was just to let her know I'd returned. There was a message on the answering machine to say my photos have arrived back at the shop, so I need to go into Llanestyn to get them. It should only take an hour or so.'

'Fine,' Heston said.

'Oh, well, if you're going in, there are one or two things — '

Kirstin began scribbling a quick list on a scrap of paper.

After a quick wash and a change,

Tani felt rather more able to face the car once more. She was thankful that neither Heston nor Kirstin had asked why she had chosen to stay at a motel last night, instead of making the journey in one go. Alys's explanation must have sounded very convincing, she concluded. The simple truth was that she had set off much later than she intended, and by the time midnight approached could scarcely keep her eyes open.

'I'm going to have to stop,' she told Alys in her last phone call.

'That's fine. I'll tell them you had a tummy-bug, a twenty-four hour kind of thing, and you'll arrive tomorrow. It'll save any awkward questions,' had been her friend's reply.

Llanestyn was a small town, with a single shopping area set around the market square. Tani picked up her photos, did a quick dash to collect the items on Kirstin's list, and made her way back to the car. It was there, while flicking through the photographs, that she discovered the last film was missing. It would be the one she had taken from Morris's field, just before she had left, the one with the best views of the entire abbey.

All kinds of possibilities shot through her mind. She remembered taking the film out of the camera and putting it in her bag. She'd been so upset that day, she hadn't noticed Morris approaching her. He could have been watching her for ages. He could even have taken the film from her bag while she had been distracted. Had she photographed something she should not have done by mistake?

Tiredness forgotten, she was deep in working out just how Morris could have removed the film without anyone noticing, when a last-minute thought had her searching through her bag. Sure enough, slipped in between a hole in the lining she had meant to fix ages ago was the missing film. Instead of being relieved, Tani cursed in a most unladylike manner.

These were the pictures she most needed to complete her painting. If she took them to the photo shop they would take another three days. There was, however, an alternative. Tani glanced at her watch. It was almost lunchtime and she had an hour for lunch. She would have just time to go into nearby Corbyn and use the one-hour processing service at the pharmacy, and be back before it became too obvious.

If anyone commented, she would just have to own up, and hope Kirstin didn't get to hear about it. It was simple. She could have lunch while she waited, and be ready and raring to go by the time she got back. She started the car, and set off.

Tani deposited her film without any problem, and set out to find a nice quiet place, with a good selection of the sweetest, stickiest, sweets going, on the principle that a good sugar hit was the best remedy for shattered nerves, and a broken heart! Since this was only the second time she had found herself in the town, her mission took some research to accomplish.

As little back streets usually offered the best bet, she followed every one she could find, until she came across a little, old-fashioned place, some way from the main streets. It was a tiny little place, with small window panes, looked most promising, and she stopped outside to inspect the menu.

'Very promising,' she said, with a quick peep inside to a half-empty room and a collection of dark, wooden tables.

Then she stopped, and peered inside once more, this time with all thoughts of meringue and chocolate cake quite vanished from her mind. There was no mistake. The girl sitting at one of the tables was definitely Alys.

Strange, Tani thought. What on earth had brought Alys here? There had been no sign of her in Llanestyn, so Tani had assumed she was already on her way back to the abbey. She smiled to herself, imagining her friend's face when she walked in. She didn't mind Alys knowing about her foolish mistake with the film, and they could have a good laugh over the whole thing together, except that it seemed it was Alys who needed the commiseration.

She had leaned forward across the table, her head in her hands, clearly in distress. Tani's instinct was to rush in immediately, but the next gesture stopped her. Someone was already providing the comforting. Long, narrow hands were gently taking those of Alys, removing them from her face, and holding them, while their owner leaned very close, speaking to her earnestly.

Morris! Alys and Morris? Surely not. Alys had defended him, said she didn't believe all the accusations against him, but that was Alys, who would never think ill of anyone. Tani turned away, and set off back as quickly as she could towards the main shopping centre. Whatever was going on, a strong instinct told her that she had seen something private, something no-one else was intended to know about.

Was Alys in some kind of trouble? She would have to watch Alys closely, try to find out all that she could without letting on what she had seen. If Alys needed help, she would do her best to protect her, or maybe Alys was beyond help. Morris, as she knew from first-hand experience, could appear understanding and sympathetic when he wanted to, charming even, charming enough to lead at least one female astray. But surely he wouldn't be trying to entangle Alys, with Heston's wife waiting for him at home, if she was waiting for him at home!

What was it that Alys herself had said? That Suzie hadn't been seen for ages, maybe not even heard of in ages. Tani swallowed. All right, she did have an over-active imagination, but what else was a girl likely to conclude from all the available facts?

But, knowing Alys, she was hardly going to listen to theories of shallow graves in Morris's back garden, not without complete and utter proof. And no-one had been known even to visit Morris at his cottage since Tani had arrived, let alone find themselves lurking in the shrubbery.

The rest of the hour had never seemed so long. Tani lurked by the shop counter for the last ten minutes, ready to grab her photographs at the earliest possible moment. It was with relief that she finally paid, and shot back to her car as quickly as she could, praying she would get back to the abbey before Alys could return to find that she had been out as well.

Something was going on, of that she was sure, something that was causing Alys the greatest of distress. Well, whatever it was, Tani determined, she was going to find out, and she was going to help her. And if Morris stood in the way, well, what did she care?

6

'Is Alys OK, do you think?' Heston asked Tani several weeks later but she replied rather evasively.

'I expect so.'

'It's just that she has seemed a little out of sorts these past few weeks,' Heston said with a frown. 'I wondered if something was bothering her.'

'I think she's just tired, that's all,' Tani replied, not quite able to meet his eyes.

They were standing in the little museum just off the courtyard, where several of the boards were now filled with information and Tani's colourful illustrations.

'Yes, maybe.'

Heston did not sound entirely convinced and Tani didn't blame him. Alys had been determinedly cheerful in the weeks since the day Tani had seen her with Morris, but it was by no means a natural cheerfulness, almost as if it were a protection around her, to avoid any questioning. Tani had never mentioned the incident. Never even, in fact, let on that she had ever been anywhere near Corbyn since her weekend away.

Since Kirstin had recently taken to staying more frequently in the room in the little apartment, protesting that she was now so busy she needed to work most evenings in the office with Heston, the two friends had found themselves with little time together for any private talk.

It felt, Tani thought sadly, as if Alys was suddenly very far away from her. All the same, she was pleased that Heston had noticed the change in her friend, too. There had been times when she had been convinced he scarcely noticed her presence at all.

'I'm sure that's all it is,' she said, as confidently as possible. 'They've scarcely stopped at the dig.'

'True.'

Heston smiled at her, his blue eyes glowing once more.

'Yes, I'm sure that must be it. She's taken such care to make sure the casket isn't damaged. I'm sure they all must be exhausted.'

'We've all been working hard.'

Kirstin looked up from putting the final touches to the last of the large boards, her eyes glittering in the beams from the spot-lights, as if accusing Tani of deliberately trying to play down the manager's contribution to the project.

'Of course,' Heston replied, turning his smile towards her. 'That's why opening the museum now is such a good idea. You are right, Kirstin, we all need some time to relax a bit. What better than an opening night party? I'm quite sure the students won't object.'

A smile came over Kirstin's neatly made-up features. Tani opted to seem engrossed in making sure her pictures had no flaws in them. Kirstin could be decidedly irritating at times, she remarked to herself, always having to be right, and the best at everything. But there was no point in alienating her. Tanwen was in no mood for a fight, and especially not with someone she would never see again after the next few weeks.

'I'll send out invitations this morning,' Kirstin said.

'I was thinking.' Heston hesitated. 'I feel I would only be fair if we invited Morris. He's been very helpful. I'm sure Alys couldn't have got on so quickly without his assistance.'

Kirstin had been pointedly watching Morris's every move each time he had come over to look at the progress of the uncovering of the casket, and to offer reassurance to Alys and her rather nervous bunch of students, all terrified of making some dire mistake which would go down for ever in the history of bungled excavations.

'I'm sure Morris has his reasons,' Kirstin replied icily.

'But he's hardly in a position to cause any harm.'

'Maybe not, but you haven't been through all that — police, auditors, staff being questioned as if they might be common criminals, not to mention picking up the pieces afterwards.'

'Of course.'

Heston looked distinctly embarrassed at this reminder of Morris's past misdemeanours. Kirstin had been through all that, Tani reflected. Kirstin had been Morris's deputy at the Heritage Centre, Alys had told her, when all the investigations into the irregularities had started. She'd had to keep the whole thing together when Morris had been suspended, not to mention facing questioning herself. Then she'd had to apply for the job of Director when Morris had been finally sacked, when she must have known that if she didn't get it the first thing a new director was likely to do was to do their best to get rid of someone who'd been there when the centre had come under such a cloud. No, it couldn't have been easy.

Tani looked at the manager with rather more sympathy than usual. No wonder Kirstin was so precise about things, after such an investigation. To her surprise, Kirstin was smiling.

'No, you're right. He can't cause any trouble, and it would look mean-spirited, if we didn't invite him after all the help he's given us. I'll send it out tomorrow.'

'I'll take it.'

Tani found herself being eyed by her two companions almost before she realised she had spoken.

'I could do with a walk. All this detailed work has given me a headache,' she added lamely.

'Really.'

Kirstin's smile made no attempt to hide her opinion as to why Tani should be so eager to go, but Heston was nodding, no such suspicion in his face.

'All right, then. I'll print it off now, and you can take it before it gets too late.'

'Fine,' Tani said.

Let Kirstin draw whatever conclusions she wanted to. Tani was not about to pass up this chance to see Morris in his own surroundings, and maybe find some hint that would unlock the key to the contradictions that clung to him. It was the best thing she could do to help Alys, she told herself, firmly.

It was a warm summer's evening as Tani set off through the gate, and past the field where she had set up her easel that day, to follow the narrow path between a group of beech trees, towards the little cottage in the distance. According to the forecast, it was the last of the fine weather for a while, and the air was still warm, with darkening clouds of a thunderstorm brooding over the distant mountains.

Despite her curiosity, Tani took her time. Kirstin was right, they had all been working as hard as they could to ensure the abbey was ready for the start of the holiday season. The builders had only just finished work on the rest of the apartments, and the smell of new paint was everywhere, mingling with the sprays and the strong glues she and Kirstin had used to finish putting together the remaining displays in the museum.

It was good to get out into the air, and feel the sun on her face. Tani made her way to the bridge with its all-too-familiar turning place, and followed the track down to the cottage.

Morris had been remarkably civilised over the past weeks, even to those, like herself, who had dared to make their way down his track, and had spent the first few days busily avoiding him. That didn't mean to say that he would be any different from before in his own territory. She was sure Heston would never have let her bring the card if he had any inkling she might have to face such embarrassment a second time, but about Kirstin, she was not so sure.

By now, however, it was too late. She was in full view of the house, and risking being spotted making a run for it was just as bad as risking her

reception when she arrived there. Tani
walked deliberately towards the door.

The cottage was small, constructed
of whitewashed stone, and with a grey
slate roof. The windows were small,
divided into old-fashioned panes, and
glinted in the evening light as if they
were carefully following every move she
made. In fact, Tani admitted, she'd had
a distinct feeling from the moment it
came in sight that she was being
watched. Still, there was nothing for it.
She rapped the knocker confidently.

'Tani!'

The door was opened almost immediately, making her more sure than ever
that he had been watching her approach.
He was dressed in an ancient pair of
jeans, definitely more for comfort than
for looks, and a baggy T-shirt. His dark
hair was tousled, almost standing on
end in places, almost as if he had been
running his hands through it in despair.
He was frowning, but at least he wasn't
yelling at her, at least, not yet.

'Anything wrong?' he asked.

'Oh, no.'

All of a sudden, Tani began to feel rather foolish. This wasn't exactly subtle, turning up like this. What must he be thinking?

'Heston wanted you to have this.'

She held out the envelope.

'It's an invitation, to the opening of the museum,' she added, as he eyed it dubiously, almost as if he expected some venomous snake to begin crawling out of its folds.

'Really? Has the lovely Kirstin resigned then?' he demanded acidly.

'No, of course not. It was Heston's idea.'

There was a moment's silence and he appeared to be rather embarrassed, and uncertain what to say next.

'I'd better be getting back,' Tani said unwillingly. 'I was just going for a walk anyhow, so I said I'd bring it over.'

'I bet Kirstin loved that,' he grunted, with a mirthless laugh. 'Straight into the pirate's den, eh?'

Her suspicions had been right. The

civilised Morris of the dig was an aberration, probably all for Alys's benefit, and any other trusting young female he might have his eye on. This was the Morris she remembered, eyes glinting at her with suspicion.

'Pirates are at sea, and it's a lion that has a den,' she retorted primly.

'Ah, yes, of course. King of the beasts. I shouldn't imagine you're expected to arrive back in one piece, you know.'

'Don't be ridiculous.'

'You're very sure of yourself.'

'Personally, I always take Hollywood thrillers with a pinch of salt,' she returned.

'Prefer love stories, then, do you?' he demanded with scorn.

Just for a moment, a flicker of pain passed over the delicate features in front of him, quickly suppressed. He saw the small chin lift a little, as if defying him to humiliate her with a reminder of that time he had found her in tears. Morris cursed to himself.

Under other circumstances . . . But it was no good going down that road. He didn't want her here. She must leave now, this moment. There was too much at stake for him to risk allowing her any closer. And yet . . .

'Sorry,' he muttered.

He was going to regret this, he could just tell.

'It's hot, you must be thirsty. I've fresh lemonade in the fridge, if you would like . . . '

For a moment, he thought his reputation had well and truly scared her off from going anywhere near his door, but then she smiled, the wide lips parting to show a gleam of even teeth, her face lighting in an almost irresistible glow. Yes, he was definitely going to regret this!

'That would be nice, thank you.'

Tani followed him inside, into a light, airy kitchen, with an old-fashioned grate in one corner, and a pine table. Doors led off into other rooms, and a staircase led up towards the next floor.

'What a lovely room!' she exclaimed. Somehow, she had expected it all to be very dark and dingy, and without any modern appliances in sight.

'It needs a lot of work,' Morris said with a grimace, as he opened the door of the fridge-freezer, and took out a jug. 'It was my grandmother's house, and her mother's before her. Gran never would let any work be done here while she was alive. It was bad enough persuading her to have running water put in, and the electrics to be connected.' He grinned. 'Part of me would like to leave it as it was, just as I remember it when I used to visit here as a kid. But it's all that city living, I'm afraid. It softens you up for things like hot water, and microwaves, and a certain lack of ice on the insides of the windows in winter. So you see, I'm not a closet romantic, after all,' he added to Tani's quizzical look.

'No need to apologise,' she returned, with a smile. 'I'm the one who was thinking of going to bed and breakfast and hang the expense, if we'd really had to sleep in that barn.'

Morris gave a quick grunt of laughter as he lifted down a couple of glasses from the shelf above the cappuccino machine, and filled them.

'So then, you know the value of creature comforts. I'm glad to hear it. I started off with such enthusiasm here, but then, well, you know how it is.'

'Oh, I know,' Tani said ruefully. 'James and I had such plans.'

She stopped, abruptly. She hadn't spoken much to anyone about James since she had been back. For a moment, she was embarrassed, but that look of understanding she remembered so well was back in his eyes, leaving any sarcasm far behind. He handed her a glass in silence, and they sipped their drinks without speaking, as if neither of them was quite sure where to take this next. It was a soft bleeping from above them that broke the spell.

'Excuse me.'

Morris leaped to his feet.

'I won't be a moment. Help yourself to biscuits. There should be some left in the tin,' he said and he disappeared up the stairs.

Tani opened the biscuit tin, but without looking inside. She was too busy taking in all she could of the room around her, while she could openly indulge her curiosity. It was clean, and very plain. The pans on the rack above the sink were clearly well-used, and the floor was spotless, and yet she could have sworn there was no sign of any woman's hand at work here. It was a very masculine place, no little nick-nacks, or bunches of flowers to brighten the starkness, except on the mantel-piece above the grate.

Tani's eyes fixed on a photograph, half hidden behind an empty letter rack. Already the bleeping had stopped, and Morris's footsteps were on the stairs, but she took in enough to make out the photograph of a very pretty young woman, beaming at the camera, holding a small child in her arms. Tani was too far away to make out the inscription scrawled at the bottom, but the line of kisses beneath was unmistakable. So much for the newly-civilised Morris. Was there no end to the man's conquests?

'Damned internet,' Morris said, returning with a smile. 'Never could get the hang of computers.'

He was lying, Tani was sure of it, just as his smile and his sympathy was a lie. Kirstin was right — he was bad news, and the sooner she got way from here the better.

'They'll be wondering where I am,' she said firmly. 'I'd better be getting back. I said I'd meet Alys for a drink,' she lied, watching his reaction to the name closely, but Morris didn't even blink.

'OK, you'd better be off then. Tell Heston thanks for the invitation.'

Morris was coming to his senses. The sooner she was out of here, the better. He'd forgotten that photo was still there, until he'd seen her eyes lingering in its direction. If she stayed, there was no telling what else her sharp gaze might spot. Even as she drained her glass and stood up, a loud creak of the floorboards above them had her turning her head upwards towards the ceiling.

'These old houses,' he said, rather too cheerfully and the look she gave him was not of one convinced.

'Really,' she replied drily.

Definitely time to get her as far away from here as possible. To his relief, his guest appeared to have exactly the same idea.

'See you,' she called, as she began to make her way back up the drive. 'And thanks for the lemonade.'

'See you at the opening.'

Old houses, my foot. There was someone up there, someone Morris had known all along was up there, listening to every word they had said. Tani forced herself to walk slowly, and to resist any temptation to look behind her. That feeling of being watched, of being closely and deliberately watched, was real, as real as anything she had ever felt in her entire life.

Whatever happened, Tani determined, flood, fire, or the end of the world, she was never, ever, coming back here again.

7

'You look as if you've escaped from bandits,' a voice interrupted her thoughts and Tani looked up as she crossed the bridge, to find a familiar figure appearing from amongst the trees.

'Not exactly,' she replied.

'Morris bite your head off, then, did he?' Lyndon resumed, with a faintly amused smile.

'No.' Tani returned his smile. Safely out of sight of the house, she was beginning to feel slightly foolish, and in no mood to have her adventures laughed over by her friends in the abbey. The less she said about the past half hour, the better, she decided.

'He was too shocked to say much.'

Lyndon laughed at this. 'And so he should be.'

He turned to walk back beside her.

'I wouldn't have let him anywhere near the place, if I was in Heston's position.'

'How did you know where I was?'

'Kirstin. She was worried about you. She knows what Morris can be like, and not just the rudeness part, if you catch my drift. He can be a tricky customer, believe me.'

'I'm sure.'

'So I was under strict instructions to rescue you, spring the trap, so to speak, if you weren't on your way back within the hour.'

'Thanks, but I made my escape on my own.'

'After a good look round?'

'Are you accusing me of being nosey?'

'Well?'

'All right. I managed a quick peep into his kitchen, but that was all, I'm afraid. It looked rather nice.'

She caught the mischievous twinkle in his eyes, and laughed.

'And, no, I didn't see any suspicious

bodies, or bottles of poison on the kitchen table.'

'Lucky he didn't offer you a cup of tea, though.'

'Very,' she returned.

No way was she about to confess she'd sat for some time drinking Morris's delicious home-made lemonade. Something told her that juicy morsel of information would get back to Kirstin, who would be sure to draw her own salacious conclusions. Tani had no intention of becoming one of Morris's seemingly endless line of conquests, and she had even less desire for any such rumour to spread. Besides, she still had hopes that Alys would one day confide in her, and so she didn't want to be seen to have any personal involvement in the matter.

'Good. I'm glad.'

She found her arm being pulled gently, but firmly, through his.

'Life here just wouldn't be the same without you.'

'Why, Lyndon!' Tani laughed. 'Are

you flirting with me?'

'Me?'

The handsome face looked at her with mock innocence.

'Never. I just appreciate the company of the prettiest young woman in the place, that's all.'

'Flattery, too. I expect you say that to every girl you meet.'

'That's the Lyndon who waves swords, and charges around in the most ridiculous get-up his director can find,' he replied ruefully. 'That Lyndon is not the real one, just the TV version. There are times I'm not sure I like him all that much.'

His eyes were suddenly serious.

'I would never hurt you, Tani, ever. I want you to believe that. I would never let any harm come to you.'

Tani looked up at him, startled at the intensity of his tone, and a little shy.

'I'm not in any danger, you know.'

'I know.'

His grip tightened just a little on her arm.

'But I wanted to tell you, all the same.'

Tani smiled up at him, and they walked back towards the abbey in companionable silence.

⋆   ⋆   ⋆

The opening party for the museum was unanimously declared a great success. The promise of the mere presence of Lyndon Hawksmoor ensured the grounds were full to bursting, for which Tani was more than thankful. With so many people, it was quite easy to avoid anyone you wished to avoid. In her case, this came down to Kirstin and Morris. Of Kirstin, she had no fear. She was too busy spending the maximum time available in the company of various celebrities to even notice the comings and goings of the lowlier members of staff. Avoiding Morris gave her more of a headache, but, in the event, he appeared only briefly, making his excuses after barely an hour before disappearing across the fields.

'Which means I can relax,' Tani said to herself, and yet, somehow, she felt ill at ease.

Yes, Tani thought to herself, as she slipped quietly away to the peace of her own room, the sooner I get out of here, and get my life back together, the better.

With the opening formally over with, there were just the last finishing touches to be completed. Tani was tempted to make the excuse of other commitments when Heston asked her to stay on for a further couple of weeks, so that she could make some preliminary sketches of the stone casket, which was, by now, almost ready to be removed to the safety of the Heritage Centre in Llanestyn. But her boss in London had already agreed, no doubt swayed by the prospect of his museum's resident historical illustrator featuring in a high-profile television series. Her own curiosity soon overcame her desire to escape.

'Besides, it's only two weeks,' she said to her mother. 'It'll be gone in a flash. What on earth can happen in two weeks?'

She might have known this was tempting fate.

'I think security is still too lax,' Kirstin said, a few days later. 'They are hoping to bring the casket out tomorrow. It is very vulnerable until we can transport it to the Heritage Centre.'

Heston frowned. He was looking pale and thin, and lines had appeared at the corners of his eyes, as if he had not been getting much sleep lately.

'Surely it can go straight away,' he replied. 'We can have the van standing by until Alys is ready.'

'I'm not having this done in a rushed manner. It will need to be packed into a crate, and well protected. It is too valuable to risk any damage to it now,' Kirstin insisted.

Heston sighed, and pressed his hand to his eyes, as if to wipe away their tiredness.

'We'll take all the care it needs,' Alys put in sharply. 'I'm quite prepared to put all the time we have into this.'

Kirstin turned to her, and eyed her with the faintest touch of scorn.

'The casket is almost free of earth already, Alys. That tarpaulin is hardly any protection against thieves or vandals. Despite all my cautioning, word has got out somehow about the uniqueness of this find. Wherever I go, I seem to hear people talking about it. It is about time we all took this more seriously. There have been enough incidents as it is.'

Alys, Tani noted with alarm, had gone completely white, and appeared on the edge of losing her temper.

'None of my students is a vandal or a thief,' she replied, with only the slightest of shakes in the cold evenness of her voice.

Kirstin shrugged, and turned away to gather up her files, signalling that the meeting was over.

'No-one has said they are,' Heston put in gently.

Alys controlled herself with an effort.

No, but the implication was there, she thought to herself, with a resentful glare towards the elegantly-retreating back of Kirstin. Several of the small brooches and pieces of pottery they had uncovered in the earth beside the casket had disappeared over the past weeks. None of them was of great value, although if the casket proved to be the one mentioned in the story, there were many collectors who would pay over the odds to have such mementos in their collections.

Security guards had been hired after the first incident, with everyone finding themselves and their vehicles searched each time they left the abbey grounds, raising an already tense atmosphere to breaking point.

'We will make sure there is extra security around the dig until the casket is safely in the museum. I'm afraid that is all we can do.'

'Would someone really steal it?' Tani asked, as she and Alys left the office and went back outside. 'I mean, wouldn't it be rather obvious if they tried to sell it? It's pretty unique, I would have thought.'

'Completely. Nothing like this has been found intact and unopened. You couldn't sell it openly, but there are collectors who would pay vast amounts to have it in their collection, particularly with the association with the story of the Ivory Princess. Things like this are often stolen to order, never to be seen again.'

'That would be awful!'

'Exactly. The casket in itself is priceless, but it's also what we find when we open it that makes it so valuable to us. If there are bones inside, it will tell us a lot about the person inside. Hopefully, we'll be able to compare the DNA with that from the bones in Prince Estyn's tomb, and see if it could be his brother, in which case it would go a long way to prove the story was based in truth.'

Enthusiasm was back in her voice, and she seemed to have put the unpleasantness of the last few minutes behind her. She turned to Tani with a smile.

'Then all we'll have to do is find the Ivory Princess.'

'I thought that was her tomb in the museum.'

'Just the tombstone, unfortunately. That is all that's ever been found. It always seemed impossible that we could ever identify her, but now there are new tests that can be done, which can show the area where someone grew up. It's to do with the level of minerals in the water,' she explained to Tani's astonished look. 'At least, it can tell the general area. People didn't generally travel so far in those days, so if we find the bones of a woman from that time who grew up in the Mediterranean, well, odds are it's something to do with the Ivory Princess.'

'Amazing.'

'Yes, it is. So no-one had better lay their hands on them.'

Her tone was fierce, almost, Tani thought, as if she was taking the petty thievery as something personal. She gave her friend an anxious look. It wasn't just the missing pieces of jewellery, she was sure of it. There had been raised voices more than once over the past few days, as if there was something here that was seriously wrong.

Part of her was relieved that there were only a few more weeks of work left. All she wanted was peace and quiet, and time to start her life again. Whatever was going on at the abbey, she had no wish to be any part of it, although, on the other hand, it would be hard to walk away from Alys, who was so clearly distressed. In fact, she realised with a sudden jolt, she was going to find it very hard to leave at all. There was something here, she admitted to herself, unwillingly, that had crept unseen into her heart, and there was a part of her that would never be able to leave.

Tani had never been so relieved to find herself with a quiet evening. Her thoughts were in a whirl, and she was in no mood for conversation. Fortunately, Kirstin was visiting her sister in Manchester for the week-end, so the little house was relaxed for once. Alys didn't seem to wish to be sociable either, so, luxuriating in the freedom from Kirstin's neat habits, and disapproving eye, the two friends cooked a leisurely supper, which they ate on their laps in the garden, even leaving the dishes for the morning.

'I wish the rain would come,' Alys sighed, rescuing the remains of a bottle of wine from the fridge, and pouring them each a glass.

'I can't sleep when it's so stuffy.'

'Me, too,' Tani agreed.

The thunderstorms had now been promised for days, but had not yet appeared, leaving the heat to build up under a clouded sky, until everything seemed to be covered with a soft film of moisture. Despite all the windows being wide open, the heat in the little house was oppressive.

'Oh, drat Kirstin,' Alys said suddenly. 'Hers are the only windows that face out of the courtyard and catch the breeze. I bet they're shut and she's locked her door again.'

They had been through this the last weekend, when Kirstin had finally gone home for a few days. Alys had been irritated to find the door locked then, but tonight her dislike of the manager was spilling over, fuelled by their earlier confrontation. With a glass of wine inside her, she was ready for action.

'What does she think she's got, the crown jewels in there?' she snapped.

Before Tani could answer, she had reached into the cupboard under the stairs, and had fished out a reel of stout wire and a pair of pliers.

'Alys! What are you up to now?'

'You'll see,' the grim reply came.

She snipped off a length of the wire,

and was up the stairs like a shot, with Tani right behind her.

'You can't do that!'

'Who says I can't?'

'Alys, it's impossible to pick a lock unless you know what you're doing. If you lose as many keys as I've done, you'll know.'

'But easy if you know how.'

'And just how many locks have you picked in your time?'

'Loads,' the unexpected reply came.

As if to prove her point, it was almost immediately followed by a grunt of triumph, and the clunk of the lock turning.

'Don't look so shocked. I don't rob banks for a living, not yet, anyhow. My dad's a locksmith. It's very lucrative.'

'I know,' Tani put in feelingly.

'He's convinced that one day I'll quit playing in mud and get a proper job, so he's forever taking me with him, when he gets a chance, and it's quite a good party piece.'

Alys was clearly enjoying herself, and

looking, in the half light, more like a child than ever.

'We all have hidden depths, you know,' she mocked gently.

Tani laughed as she followed her into the room. There was definitely more to Alys than met the eye, she thought to herself with a smile. Perhaps that had all been nothing with Morris after all. Maybe it had just been work getting on top of her, and Morris had just been at the right place at the right time. This might still sound like too much of a coincidence, but of one thing she felt certain — Kirstin could have more of a fight than she imagined on her hands when it came to Heston.

'That's better.'

Alys opened the windows, allowing a faint breeze to enter.

'I'll lock it tomorrow morning, and she'll be none the wiser.'

Of course, they couldn't quite help having a quick look around. A few bits of make-up stood on the dressing-table, but otherwise there was no sign that the room had ever been slept in.

'I don't think there would be any stolen goods here.'

Tani smiled, catching a definite meaning in her friend's careful scrutiny.

'We could always plant some,' she added.

'Alys!' Tani exclaimed.

'Only joking. Well, almost only joking. I'd just like to wipe that superior look off her face, just once. But it might be just a bit obvious.'

'Just a bit,' Tani agreed.

She made a mental note to make sure she was there when Alys locked the door again. She was sure her friend wasn't serious, but there was no harm in making sure she didn't give in to temptation in the night!

'Come on, that wine will be getting warm at this rate.'

★   ★   ★

It was still dark when Tani woke. It must be nearing dawn, she thought, peering at the clock beside her bed. Just the faintest hint of light was stealing in between the curtains. It was still just as humid, and she could have sworn she heard a deep rumble of thunder in the distance. She was too hot, and she was thirsty.

Unwillingly, she dragged herself out of bed and tiptoed her way on to the landing. Everything was quiet, and, not wanting to disturb Alys, she decided not to put on the light, but to feel her way down to the kitchen. The door to Kirstin's room was still wide open, allowing the breeze, now a little stronger and cooler, to waft through the house. Once again, there came the distant rumble of thunder.

Without thinking, Tani made her way to the window of Kirstin's room. She was not particularly fond of thunderstorms, but the cool air was irresistible. As she peered out, the rumble came again, this time accompanied by a flash of light, but this was no thunderstorm.

Tani blinked, and stared as hard as she could.

There was another flash of light, but like the first one, it did not originate in the sky, but on the ground, amongst the fields, and in the direction of the dig! It must be the security men, she remembered suddenly, with relief. She was about to turn away when the strange sound came again. Her eyes could just make out something, something that looked like a vehicle, making its way over the field from Morris's land. The rumble, she realised, was caused by the tyres slipping on the rough ground.

Surely Kirstin's suspicions couldn't have been correct all along. Surely Morris would never be so stupid, or so desperate. She swallowed. Another thought had hit her — that memory of Alys, in tears, and Morris holding her hand, comforting her, or perhaps persuading her, or blackmailing her! Tani stepped out on to the landing. There was no sound from Alys's room, not even a hint of breathing. Maybe she wasn't in there at all. Maybe she was out in the field, helping Morris, willingly, or otherwise, in some nefarious scheme or other.

Of course, she could be wrong, but even if the door was unlocked, just trying to open it could wake Alys, and that would drag Alys into this whole thing. There could be some perfectly innocent explanation, and her imagination was off again, running away with her.

There was only one way to find out. Tani crept back into her room without the faintest thought of calling the police, found her jumper and her mobile phone, and, with her shoes in her hand, stole downstairs, and out.

8

Outside, the grass was damp beneath her feet. Tani slipped on her shoes, and went through the garden as fast as she could. The door opened without a sound, and she ran towards the ruins of the abbey, faintly visible, silhouetted against the lightening sky.

She reached the ruins without incident, and, feeling safer in the shadows of the huge pillars, began to make her way towards Alys's trench, and the small shed that had housed the casket for the night. The sounds were still there, she noted, with a sinking feeling in the pit of her stomach. They were louder now, with the faint murmur of voices every now and again. Strangely, no-one seemed to be about in the abbey. What about the security guards? The answer came as she reached the last pillar. As she reached out to guide herself by the cool stone, her feet tripped over something large and soft, nearly sending her flying.

It was definitely human. A tentative hand reaching out told her that much. He was lying on one side, his breathing slow and heavy. A small shake confirmed that the security guard was unconscious, and, by the feel of things, about as firmly trussed up as he could be. Tani swallowed. This was either an elaborate joke, or it was real.

She peered cautiously round the edge of the pillar, with an uneasy conviction that this was real, and the sooner she got out of here and started using her mobile, the better. The light was improving by now, and her brief scan of the scene showed a van backed up as near to the shed as possible, while dark figures were attempting to manhandle a very large and unwieldy case towards its open back.

'Move it, will you? We haven't got all day.'

'Give us a chance, Lennie. It's heavy.'

She concluded, with a mixture of anxiety and relief, none of the voices was familiar, and they were struggling to get the casket to the van.

The argument before her was growing more heated. The casket, it seemed, was a good deal more unwieldy than the thieves had expected, and tempers were being frayed. She turned to make her way back to a safe place to phone the police, and then alert Heston and the others, but next moment, her resolve was distracted by the driver of the van.

'It's taking too long,' he said sharply. 'Another ten minutes and it'll start to get light. We should be out of here.'

At the first word, Tani turned back, grabbing at the pillar to support herself. Inside her, she felt as if her heart had died. The driver was none other than Morris!

'We're doin' our best. You want it in one piece, don't you?'

'Of course. I also want to get out of here in one piece, if you don't mind.'

123

'OK, OK, mate. Keep your hair on.'

Beside her, the security guard began to stir. For one moment, Tani had an urge to bash him over the head, anything to make sure the thieves escaped. She no longer cared about the casket. She no longer cared about anything. When she looked back again, the wooden box was being loaded at last into the back of the van. It was too late for her to phone anyhow. A few more moments, and they'd be gone. The security guard moved again, this time letting out a low groan. This time, a wild fury coursed through Tani's veins.

All right, so she might have been a soft-headed idiot, but no more. She could make out the guard more clearly now. He looked very young. She bent down until her lips were as close to his nearest ear as possible.

'Ssh,' she whispered. 'Just keep still. They haven't gone yet. I'll get help.'

To her relief, she sensed him give a brief nod, and his struggling ceased. In a moment Tani was running back towards the safety of the next pillar. She might have known she would never make it. It had been in the back of her mind that the looters were lax in the look-out department, and she had hoped against hope that this was a sign of them being rank amateurs, until a large form stepped out from the shadow of the pillar and grabbed her.

This was one time when heels might have been useful, but she did her best to inflict as much damage as possible with her trainers. They made little impression, but when a hand was placed over her mouth, her teeth definitely found their mark.

'You little — '

Her assailant cursed aloud. Tani found herself being dragged, still struggling, back towards the main group. If she'd ever wanted an audience in her life, she had one now. Each one of them stopped in their work to stare at her in the fast-growing light. She stopped wriggling, being as it was useless anyhow, and less than dignified, and glared as balefully as she could at her captors.

'Must be from the house,' the man holding her muttered. 'I was following her for ages.'

Liar, Tani thought, but she had the sense not to voice this aloud, and let them know that she had been watching them for a while. The casket was now in the van, and the doors shut. Maybe they would think she believed they were just poachers, she wondered hopefully, although they'd know that once the theft had been discovered she'd soon put two and two together.

She swallowed hard, and tried not to think what the next few hours might hold. She still had her phone in her pocket. If she could just reach it before they searched her. She tried to visualise where the number nine was positioned on the keys. Surely they'd be able to trace her, even if she only reached the emergency service for a few minutes. She stood as still as she could, and waited for her chance. Lennie, a burly man who appeared to be the leader was cursing at some length.

'So now what do we do?' he demanded at last, looking at the captive as if he had every desire to throttle her there and then.

Behind Lennie, Tani caught a glimpse of the driver making his way purposefully towards them. She shut her eyes, and wished, as she had never wished before, that she was still safely tucked up in bed.

'Leave her to me,' the driver said gruffly. 'I'll deal with her.'

Lennie let out a meaningful guffaw.

'One of yours then, is she, Morris?'

'Yes.'

Tani's eyes shot open. Her first impulse was to pull away as he grasped hold of her arm, but then a strong sense of self-preservation reasserted itself. Whatever Morris might be, she had an instinct she had a better chance of worming her way out of this mess with him than if she was bundled into the van with the rest of them. His face, she saw, was drawn and gaunt in the grey light. His eyes sought hers with something like a pleading in their dark depths, and maybe even a reflection of the fear now coursing through her. The mood around her, she could feel, had changed. Whatever intent lay behind the eyes that watched her, she didn't like to think.

'Damn her, she's got a phone.'

The man who had grabbed her had been in the process of letting her go, a little unwillingly, at a curt signal from his boss. His hands, lingering just a little longer than was necessary over her body, had come into contact with her pocket.

'I haven't used it,' Tani said quickly.

She pulled out the offending article before anyone could use it as an excuse to manhandle her further.

'She's lying.'

'No, look,' Morris said as he removed the phone from her grasp. 'It shows you the last call made. See? It's a London code. No emergency number I've ever heard of.'

There was a brief muttering. Morris rapidly opened the back of the phone and detached the memory card, and flung it into the deep shadows of the trench at their feet, stuffing the useless phone into his own pocket.

'No harm done, OK?'

'Brute!' she muttered.

'You'll thank me,' he replied harshly, taking a firmer grip on her arm.

At least, Tani thought, Alys didn't appear to be a part of this. She was sure her friend would never have kept quiet if she was there and had seen her. At least Morris hadn't been able to persuade her to this, whatever else he had done.

'Come on, it's nearly light. Let's get out of here.'

'I'm not so sure.'

Tani's stomach contracted at the tone in Lennie's voice.

'She's seen us. She can identify us.'

'D'you think I don't know that?'

Morris said tersely. 'Like I said, I'll deal with it.'

'I prefer to clear up my own mess,' the ominous reply came. 'Leave no room for error.'

Tani found the gleaming barrel of a small but businesslike gun pointed straight in her direction. She felt Morris's grasp change on her arm.

'Don't be an idiot,' he snapped. 'No-one's going to give a toss about a piece of old stone. Add murder, and they'll never give up.'

'I like my messes clean,' the stubborn reply came.

The next moment, all hell broke loose. Tani was aware of Morris shouting, and of noise erupting all around her, and above it all, the nearby crack as a gun was fired. She had no time to react. She was vaguely aware of Morris turning her, so that her body was shielded by his, and pushing her towards the steep sides of the trench. The next moment, they were falling, clasped tightly together as they slid in the earthy darkness at the bottom of the pit.

'Morris?' Tani said in a tentative whisper.

He was lying half across her, and very still. She had fully expected a hail of bullets to follow them, but no-one had even so much as peered over the sides of the trench. Whatever was happening above was keeping all those involved fully occupied. She could still hear the shouts, and see the sweep of powerful torches across the top of the hole in which they lay. In the far distance she could hear the blare of a police siren, several sirens in fact, coming rapidly nearer.

'Morris? Are you OK?'

She had no wish to move, but a quick surveying of herself left her with the impression that she was unhurt. In the light reflected from the torches, she could see a dark stain oozing across the surface of her jumper.

'Morris!'

To her relief, he stirred.

'Morris, you're hurt. You're bleeding all over me.'

'Am I?'

He moved the arm flung over her and cursed.

'That idiot actually hit me. Must have been a lucky shot.'

'He was aiming at me,' Tani reminded him.

'He never did have good taste,' he murmured.

His face was very close to hers, and unless she pushed him bodily away from her, there was not a lot she could do about.

'Here.'

She wriggled a little, and managed to extract a handkerchief from her pyjama pocket.

'You're lucky. My grandmother gave me them last Christmas. It's not exactly clean, though,' she added grimly.

'That's OK.'

His warm breath brushed her face, and there was the stirrings of a laugh in his voice.

'So long as you nurse me.'

'In your dreams, Morris,' she retorted.

He was so close, he almost enveloped her. Inside her, she felt her heart clench.

'You saved my life,' she added in a rather gentler tone.

'Did I? That must be worth something then.'

Tani swallowed. This couldn't be happening. This whole evening must be a dream. She couldn't be here, lying in Morris's arms at the bottom of Alys's muddy trench, while the sounds of a mad chase erupted on the ground above them.

'The police came,' she said, in a rather desperate attempt to bring them both back to reality.

Morris scarcely seemed to hear her. His lips were gently brushing the portion of her face nearest to him, travelling slowly but surely towards her mouth which, under other circumstances . . .

'They'll arrest you,' she said to distract him.

'Morris! Will you stop that, and listen to me!'

'Not a chance.'

'This is all my fault. You were in the van. You could have made it. You could have escaped.'

That had the effect of stopping him.

'Does that matter to you, Tani?'

'No, of course not.'

'Sure?'

His face was very close, and the searching lips were back, this time finding the corner of her mouth. One more torment, and he'd have his answer anyway.

'Yes, no. Oh, damn you, Morris! Of course it matters. And now I'll never see you again. Now will you leave me alone.'

To her horror, her voice was suddenly shaking with tears.

'Tani,' he whispered. 'Tani, don't cry.'

'You all right, miss?'

A powerful beam was abruptly directed on the two of them, as a policeman inspected his find, with more than the usual show of interest, which, given appearances, Tani suddenly realised was no wonder.

'Yes, fine.'

'Just step away from the young lady, will you, sir?' the officer resumed in blandly formal tones.

'He can't,' Tani said. 'He's hurt. He's been shot.'

The beam lingered on their huddled forms just a moment longer, as if to establish Morris did not have a gun at her head, and then wavered a little as the policemen turned to shout to his colleagues across the field.

'Write to me.'

Morris's voice was urgent in her ear.

'Write to me, Tani. There are things I want to tell you. Things I can't say here. Please.'

Tani looked at the drawn face, the brows now furrowed in pain, and another emotion she didn't dare think upon. Figures were sliding down beside them. She winced at the sharp intake of breath as his arm was lifted away from her. Then she was aware of strong hands holding her, telling her everything would be all right, and beginning to lift her out of the trench.

'Tani!' she heard Morris call after her, and she just managed to twist her face towards him briefly.

'Yes,' she replied.

9

The next few weeks were the emptiest of Tani's life. Everyone was very kind, but inside, she felt numb. She got through the police interviews, and the questions from her friends in a daze.

Fortunately, no-one seemed to have the heart to start work on the casket, now safely stored in Llanestyn Heritage Centre, and most of her other work had been completed. Most of the time, she felt as if she sleep-walked through each day, not quite sure what exactly she had done.

'Why don't you write to him?' Alys demanded.

She seemed to have taken the entire affair in her stride, as if she were accustomed to attempted robberies of priceless artefacts on a daily basis. Under her gentle questioning, Tani had given a brief outline of the night's adventures, tactfully leaving out most of the events at the bottom of the trench, and earning herself an old-fashioned look from her friend.

'Sounds like Morris wanted to give you an explanation. Give him a second chance, Tani. I know it doesn't look good.'

'Understatement of the century, or what, Alys?'

'All right. It looks really bad, but no-one is ever completely wicked, you know. Maybe he did have a reason, however mistaken. I'm sure he has some kind of explanation.'

'Don't they all?' Tani growled, and Alys left the subject well alone.

The atmosphere in the abbey was not exactly calculated to lift her mood. Heston was grim, with scarcely a word for anyone. It seemed he had taken Morris's arrest almost as hard as the attempted robbery. He scarcely commented when messages came through from the relieved staff in the Heritage Centre that the burial casket appeared to be unharmed by its unexpected adventures, and promised many exciting discoveries to be found. The tension was made no easier by Kirstin, who stalked the buildings.

'I told you so,' seemed to ring from every tap of her high-heeled shoes, shredding Tani's remaining nerves into little pieces.

'She looks like she owns the place,' she muttered, almost to herself.

On the morning of her final day at the abbey, Tani looked up from her half-hearted attempts to finish her last painting, to find Lyndon standing a few paces away, watching her intently.

'Who does?'

'Kirstin.'

'Oh, yes, I suppose so. She's got every right. She did warn everyone.'

He scarcely seemed to have heard her.

'Heston seems to have given into her. Have you seen how he always defers to her now?'

Tani sighed.

'I don't blame him. All this must have dented his confidence.'

She pulled herself together.

'Not much for you to film any more, I'm afraid.'

'Oh, that's OK.'

He reached her in a few strides, and sat down on the step beside her.

'We'd got all we needed for this series anyhow, and quite a bit of drama besides. Are you still sure you don't want to be interviewed about it? You were quite the heroine, you know.'

'No, thanks.'

'That's OK. I told them you'd made up your mind, so they're not expecting it.'

'Thanks. You've been very kind.'

'Kind, my foot. My director just wants the chance to put me in the position of knight errant, that's all.'

For all the humour in his voice, his eyes were serious.

'Instead, that fell to Morris, after all.'

'He saved my life,' Tani said. 'Whatever he is, and whatever he has done, I'll never forget that.'

He watched her in silence, as she struggled against tears.

'I'm sorry,' she said at last. 'I'm being silly. It was just a bit of a shock, that's all. Not what you expect in a quiet place like this.'

Lyndon winced as the tears threatened to overwhelm her.

'Everything I touch seems to go bad,' she muttered. 'First James . . . '

Her voice died away, and she struggled to find a handkerchief.

'Take no notice. I'm just feeling sorry for myself, it will be gone in a bit.'

She found her free hand being taken gently.

'Don't be sorry, Tani,' he said, gently and kindly. 'This is not your mess. You must never think that.'

He gently brushed the tear-dampened tendrils of hair from her face.

'None of this is your fault.'

'Doesn't excuse my bad judgement though, does it?' she retorted bitterly, tears beginning to escape once more.

'Maybe you were right in the first place, that day we met in the abbey. Maybe I should have been a nun, and spent my life in good deeds.'

Both her hands were held captive now. He lifted them to his lips.

'Clever, beautiful, Tani, I don't honestly think you were ever cut out to be a nun, good deeds or not.'

A faint smile appeared on his face as Tani sniffed, in an unlady-like fashion. Her lips, though not particularly rosy at this moment, were irresistible. He leaned a little closer.

'I wish I could see you happy again,' he murmured.

Whatever his intentions, he found himself interrupted by the pointed clearing of a throat near to them. Lyndon gave a rueful smile.

'Maybe I will, one day,' he said, brushing Tani's lips briefly with his own, then releasing her hands, and getting to his feet. 'Nice day,' he called cheerfully to Alys, who was watching the pair with folded arms.

'I've seen better,' she returned, in an unmistakably frosty manner.

Lyndon winced, and for a moment the two eyed each other, not unlike boxers about to step into the ring. Alys barely came up to the presenter's shoulder, and had never wielded a sword in her life, but it was Lyndon who dropped his gaze first. He said something quickly, too low for Tani to hear, and strode rapidly between the buildings, and out of sight.

'He was only trying to be kind,' Tani protested.

'I'm sure.'

Alys unfolded her arms and came to join her.

'Nearly finished?'

'Yes, I suppose so. I can't seem to get this last bit right.'

'Leave it then. Finish it tomorrow, before you leave.'

'Suppose so,' Tani said, with the beginnings of a smile.

'Good. Then you can come with me.'

'Where are you going?'

Tani eyed the large bag slung over Alys's shoulder.

'To Morris's house.'

She met her friend's startled look, and continued.

'I promised I'd pick up some things for him. I'm going on to visit him afterwards. You can come with me, if you want.'

'I don't think so.'

'Come on, Tani. They're moving him tomorrow, and this might be your last chance to speak to him.'

She saw the hesitation, and threw in her trump card.

'After all, he did save your life.'

'That's not fair, Alys.'

'Who said life was fair? At least come to the house.'

'OK.'

Alys seemed to be afraid Tani might change her mind again, and was suddenly all in haste to get off.

'We can go through the fields. I can pick up the car later.'

She began to pack away Tani's

brushes and crayons.

'You can leave these ir
No-one will disturb the

Slightly bemused, Tan
being organised and propen
the gate and the little path she h
once before.

'Alys, what are you up to?' she asked
anxiously.

'Up to? Me? Nothing.'

'Oh, yes?'

'You need some fresh air.'

'I was in the fresh air,' Tani insisted.

'And a change of scene.'

'I could go into the mountains for
that, or to the beach.'

'Fine. We can do that tomorrow.'

There was a sparkle in Alys's eyes
that hadn't been there since she had
picked Kirstin's lock that night. Tani
had a feeling she was thoroughly
enjoying herself. She herself wasn't
looking forward to finding herself at the
house once more. Even though she had
only been there once in her life, it was
full of memories. But there was no time

...к. With Alys's relentless pace, soon found themselves in front of house.

'The police are here!' Tani insisted, uneasy at the sight of several police cars and vans drawn up in the drive.

'It's OK. They're just cleaning out some of Morris's stuff, computers, that sort of thing. They know I'm coming.'

Alys stopped in front of the door, squared her shoulders, as if gearing up for a fight, and knocked. After a few moments it was opened a little way.

'Alys Harmon, I phoned earlier.'

'Yes, of course. Come this way, miss.'

The door opened fully, revealing a young police officer. Tani felt her cheeks begin to flame, as his scrutiny passed beyond Alys towards her. There was no mistake. It was the same one who had shone the torch down into the trench that night, to discover her and Morris cuddled up together like a pair of love-sick teenagers.

'I'm not sure,' he began.

'She's with me,' Alys said, pushing

past him in a determined manner.

Small as she was, Alys was not one to let anything stand in her way, once she'd put her mind to something. The sergeant stood and floundered, and then followed them into the kitchen.

'I'm sorry, miss, I just don't think I can allow her to accompany you.'

'Like I said, she's with me.'

His mouth opened, and then closed again, as if at a total loss as how to deal with this unexpected invasion. The kitchen was much as Tani had seen it last time, perhaps a few more mugs on the table, and the sound of voices in the distance, but otherwise clean and neat, just as if it were expecting its owner to return and start cooking dinner at any moment. Tani felt her breath catch in her throat. She couldn't bear to be here.

'It's OK. I'll wait outside,' she said.

'No, you won't,' Alys said loud and firm. 'You're staying here with me.'

She turned to the officer.

'Tani is a friend of Morris.'

He did try to remain professional, but the eyes couldn't quite hide the scepticism at the description as friend, setting Tani's face alight once more, with a wish for Alys to just shut up, and allow her to sink through the floor. But if anything, Alys was speaking even louder.

'She wanted to come with me. I was sure no-one would mind.'

Had her friend gone entirely mad? Did she want the entire law enforcement contingent of the area to hear their conversation? Tani looked at her in bewilderment, determined more than ever to run at the slightest chance. But before she could make a move, there was a creak on the stairs above them, and a familiar voice was saying, 'It's OK, sergeant.'

Tani looked up, with a certainty that the world had gone quite mad, and with a vow never to try to use that imagination of hers in the future, ever. But there was no mistaking the man making his way down the stairs, left arm heavily bandaged and secured in a sling.

'Morris!' she exclaimed.

'Come on, officer, she's not doing any harm,' Morris continued.

'She shouldn't be here.'

'Well, it's a bit late for that now, isn't it?'

'I've brought you all a cake,' Alys put in brightly, with the sweetest of smiles. 'I thought you might need it.'

The sergeant cleared his throat, obviously knowing he was defeated. Morris had reached the bottom step.

'Please, John,' he was pleading, 'five minutes. You can sling all of us in the cells afterwards, if you want.'

'Five minutes,' came the grudging reply. 'And no funny business.'

Before she could open her mouth, Tani found Morris had grasped her hand in his good one, and was hauling her up the stairs.

10

'Morris, what are you doing here? Why aren't you . . . ' Tani stammered as they reached the top of the stairs.

'In leg irons, on death row, waiting for the scaffold to be finished?'

'This is not funny, Morris.'

'Sorry.'

'No, you're not.'

Indeed, he was grinning away as if he was thoroughly enjoying her bewilderment. All around them, in the small back bedroom of the cottage, computer screens blinked away quietly.

'All right, I'm not in the least, especially since Alys took it into her head to bring you here, rather than drag you off into Corbyn like she'd agreed. I just hope Heston knows what he's letting himself in for.'

'And you'd know, I suppose,' she snapped, all the pent-up emotion of the past weeks coming out in something approaching a snarl.

The grin vanished, instantly.

'No, of course not, Tani. What d'you think I am?'

'I don't know. I'm not sure.'

'There you are, you see. I can soon explain.'

'I saw you,' she interrupted sharply. 'It's no good. I saw you and Alys in the café in Corbyn, the day I got back. You were holding her hand.'

She looked up to find his gaze resting thoughtfully on her.

'Now that sounds like a jealous woman to me.'

'Don't flatter yourself. I just don't want any more of your lies, that's all.'

'So why didn't you ask Alys about it, if it bothered you that much?'

'Oh, please. When she'd told me all about that business with Heston's wife, and there was that woman in the photograph downstairs.'

She stopped, felling herself growing more beetroot shade by the minute.

What had got into her? She did sound like a jealous woman. She looked up, expecting to find him furious, but instead discovered he was looking at her in some alarm.

'Good gracious, Tani, you don't think I've got that kind of energy, do you? You're in for a bit disappointment, if you do.'

Despite herself, Tani giggled.

'That's better.'

His good hand reached towards her, as if irresistibly drawn.

'Look, Alys and I . . . ' he began. 'There is no Alys and I. Whatever kind of degenerate you might think I am, you don't honestly think Alys has got eyes for anyone but Heston, do you?'

'Well, no.'

'There you are, then. Alys came to me for help. I never thought anyone would find us there. Thank goodness it was you, and not — well, anyhow, thank heaven it was only you who saw us.'

'Alys came to you for help? To steal her precious casket, I suppose?'

'No, of course not. She was worried. There were things happening at the abbey, little things, nothing you could put your finger on, but put together they didn't make a very nice picture.'

'But why you?'

'They were the same sorts of things — things from the dig disappearing, bits of money vanishing from the accounts, small inefficiencies, that sort of thing — all similar happenings at the Heritage Centre before all the trouble there, only this time, it was all pointing to her precious Heston. We've always got on, Alys and I, and she never did believe all the things I was accused of. So she concluded the same thing was going to happen to Heston, and maybe if I helped her sort it out, I could clear my own name, too.'

'Oh. So did you agree to help her?'

'Not exactly.'

'What d'you mean?'

'Well, all that evidence against me at the centre was very clever, you know. No way could you have proved otherwise. The police said as much themselves at the time. The only thing was I'd always had this little fantasy going around in my head.'

'I'm not sure I want to hear this.'

'Not that kind of fantasy, you fool. You know, boy's stuff — James Bond, that sort of thing.'

A tiny light was beginning to dawn in Tani's brain, while her heart began to pound in a perfectly unreasonable manner.

'And I am an expert, you know, on mediaeval artefacts.'

'Morris, don't tell me you're a complete fraud, and you've been working with the police all along.'

'Well, there had been some thefts of mediaeval paintings several years ago — theft, international fraud, dodgy collectors. I was a logical choice to help out on the expertise front, and I couldn't miss a chance like that.'

'But, Morris, everyone thinks — '

'Well, that was the idea, of course. Either it came out that I'd been helping the authorities on the quiet for years, or I took the chance to have the best cover story going to catch the real brains behind it all. What would you do?'

'Well.'

'Exactly. You'd do the same. I knew it, it's why we're perfect for each other, of course.'

'Morris!'

'I must admit, I had a whale of a time at first. I'd been working abroad before my grandmother left me this cottage, and I got the job at the Heritage Centre, so no-one here knew me very well, except for Heston, and he wasn't speaking to me by then. I'd had trouble with kids on my land, breaking fences, scaring the sheep, the usual kind of kids' stuff. So I had no problems becoming the evil recluse. To be honest, I was so fed-up with everything that had gone on here, I was looking forward to finishing the job, and starting a new life elsewhere. I'm still glad it's all over. Being the local villain can get very tiresome after a while, especially when the most gorgeous woman you have ever laid eyes on appears on your track, and starts telling you what she thinks of you, and all you want to do is tell her you positively ache to spend the rest of your life with her.'

'Don't change the subject.'

'Change the subject? Me? Do I look as if I've changed the subject?'

Tani frowned at him, trying her best to keep that treacherous heart of hers from banging away like that beneath her T-shirt.

'So there was someone up here, that time.'

'Ah, yes, the unfortunate, creaking floorboards. I didn't think you'd missed that one. John never was light-footed.'

'John? You mean the sergeant down there?'

'That's the one. He's keeper of the surveillance equipment, and general bodyguard.'

'But they arrested you,' she said.

'Better that way. Don't you see?'

He leaned forward, eyes suddenly earnest.

'They might have been a bunch of clowns out there, but they are no joking matter. I'll need to keep my head down for a while as it is. If they thought I'd been sent out to trap them, not work for them — '

There was a moment's silence. He took her hands in his, and this time she made no protest.

'I couldn't believe it when they dragged you out that night. I never meant anyone to be harmed, least of all you. The police were waiting to catch them red-handed. A few more minutes, and it would have all been over. When I saw you there, well, that's when I knew I couldn't carry on with that any longer. I'm not James Bond, Tani. I really am a boring archaeology professor who loved scrabbling about in old rubbish tips, and going home to my wife and children.'

Even one-handed, he was managing to pull her off her seat a little closer towards him.

'I just need the wife and children,' he whispered, as his lips came into contact with the lobe of her ear, but, despite a very strong temptation, Tani was not ready to give in yet.

'Suzie,' she said, accusingly, stepping away from his embrace.

'Ah, Suzie, dear Suzie. Well, she's not here, not even under the floorboards, if that's what you're thinking.'

'I'm not!'

'Yes, you are. Haven't you ever considered a change of profession, and taken up writing thrillers?'

'No, of course not. I'd never sleep. I can't even read one without seeing murderers behind every tree.'

She caught his grin, and frowned.

'And stop changing the subject.'

'Did you know you look irresistibly pretty when you're angry?'

'Morris!'

'Suzie is alive and well, and living in Eastbourne, and sending me photographs to prove it.'

He reached out behind one of the

computer screens, and lifted the photo she had seen on the mantelpiece. She did try not to, but she couldn't quite help peering at it again, attempting to make out any familiarity in the features of the small boy.

'No, he's not mine,' Morris growled.

'I didn't say so.'

'You were about to, but if you really want to know, she did sleep in that bed, for one night only — alone.'

'I don't want to think about it, thank you.'

'Well, you're going to. It wasn't a mistake, or something I regret, apart from the stiff neck and the bad back I had next day from sleeping in the chair, making sure she didn't try anything foolish.'

He met her slightly shocked gaze, and his tone softened.

'Suzie was never meant for a life like this. She loves the town, parties, being able to go out and meet friends and have loads of children. Heston can get so wrapped up in his work at times.

Well, she was in a proper state when I found her, struggling through that stream of mine. To be honest, if there had been any heavy rain and the pools had been deep, well, I don't like to think what might have happened. She was adamant she didn't want to go back to Heston, so I did the only thing I could think of. I dosed her up with a couple of whiskies, let her sleep here, and then drove her to her mother's the next day. She got treatment, and she's fine now. Got married last year, in fact, and had Daniel. She's in her element.'

'Oh,' Tani said blankly. 'Does Heston know?'

'Have you never heard of phones, e-mails and good, old-fashioned post?' he returned. 'Of course, Heston knows. In a way, that makes it worse. If he'd ever believed all those rumours were true, that would have just meant I was wicked, and it was all my fault. What he hates is that Suzie felt she had to come to someone else when she was in trouble. I don't think he can ever quite forgive himself for that. And then Suzie had me down as some kind of guardian angel, all wings and halos. Heaven knows what Heston will do when he hears the latest, and just when we were beginning to be on speaking terms again.'

'Which is?'

Morris cleared his throat.

'She wants me to be godfather to Daniel,' he replied. 'Well, that's my career as a minor criminal over with, for a start.'

'You could always say no.'

'Mm.'

'Morris! You're a total sham. You wouldn't give it up for the world.'

'Maybe not,' he admitted with grin, 'and it did get me thinking, mainly how I'd like even more to be looking for godparents for my own children. It must be because I'd also met this gorgeous, sexy, live-wire of a woman.'

'You can't just order a wife. This is not the Middle Ages. And anyhow, look what happened to Prince Estyn when he tried.'

'Oh, don't worry. I'm a new man. Persuasion is much more fun, much as I'd like to sling you over one shoulder.'

'Morris, will you please be serious.'

A sudden thought struck her.

'They've all gone very quiet down there.'

'Come on, Tani, you don't think the local constabulary is averse to a happy ending, do you? It didn't pass unnoticed that you were holding me quite unnecessarily tight that night. If you don't say yes, you're likely to find yourself arrested, you know.'

Tani felt her cheeks burn. Below, the loud chatter was almost instantly resumed, with the clatter of plates and cups being cleared away.

'It must be more than five minutes,' she added hastily, to cover her confusion.

'It's all right. Now you're here, you can stay. The idea was not only to bring you here, but it was to get you out of the abbey for the rest of the day. We all felt you'd been through enough police raids as it was.'

'But they arrested everybody that

night,' Tani said anxiously.

New possibilities were coursing through her addled brain, and she wasn't sure she liked any of them.

'Which included me,' Morris replied. 'We were just the fall-guys, Tani, dispensable if we messed up. There were more brains behind this, the ones with no trail leading to them.'

He gestured towards the window.

'See.'

Through the trees, Tani could just make out a small convoy of police cars making their way along the driveway to the abbey.

'A short while, and it will all be over.'

'Lyndon knew.'

The half-heard words suddenly fell into place.

'That's what he said to Alys this morning — get her out of here.'

'Did he now,' Morris replied thoughtfully. 'He must have changed his mind then. I'm glad. For all his faults, Lyndon is too good a communicator to be dragged down by something like this.'

'He was always trying to tell me something,' Tani said. 'I wish I'd listened more, but Kirstin always seemed to get in the way.'

'Ah. That's where I have a small confession to make,' Morris said.

'Am I going to like this?'

'Probably not. You see, you were too busy having me seducing half the women in the locality to spot the only one I really had been involved with.'

'Kirstin?'

Tani jumped back, putting as much space between them as she could manage within the small room, the only temptation left within her being a desire to damage his shins in any way possible.

'You and Kirstin? Morris, how could you?'

'I was young. I was foolish and I was seriously flattered. It was a long time ago, when we were students. I just couldn't believe that this glamorous creature wanted to go out with me. It was before Lyndon Hawksmoor and his sword-waving made grubbing around in muddy trenches a cool thing to do. And anyhow, my friends were quick to point out Kirstin never even looked in my direction until I'd published a book that had loads of people wanting to interview me for the national Press and the TV, and she was only interested in draping herself around me when the cameras were there.'

Tani winced at the brief shadow of remembered humiliation that crossed his features.

'So the upshot of it all was that she began to get serious, and I finished with her. I was angry, and I don't suppose I was very nice about it.'

He gave out a snort of grim amusement.

'How was I to know Kirstin has a very long memory, and enough ambition to sink a battleship? When she applied for the job at the Heritage Centre she'd had a dazzling career in TV history programming, and I assumed the past had been long forgotten, just as Lyndon must have thought all her pulled strings to get him his own series so quickly would never require favours returned, especially not of the dirty work for the black-naming of people like me and Heston.'

'Poor Lyndon.'

'Poor Lyndon, except if he's finally decided to break free of Kirstin and give evidence on everything that's happened. He'll probably be let off reasonably lightly, and I don't expect his image will suffer from a whiff of real danger hanging around him.'

Morris sighed, a little ruefully.

'I'm afraid I'm the one who caused all this. If I'd just confronted Kirstin at the Centre, instead of letting her think she'd got away with it, she'd probably never have set her sights on Heston's job as well, and ended up in quite such a mess. I never thought she'd be so reckless as to get mixed up with the local underworld in her attempts to discredit Heston.'

'Morris, she'd have made it impossible for you ever to work as an archaeologist again,' Tani said, shivering.

'That's where any sympathy for her does fade rapidly,' he replied with the glimmerings of a smile.

'But, Morris, Kirstin wasn't even here that night, and her mobile was switched off. Alys said they had to get her sister out of bed to get hold of her. So she had to be in Manchester.'

'With her sister, who just happens to be a solicitor. Best alibi you could get. Kirstin.always was a stickler for details. Whatever happened, you can be sure Kirstin intended coming out of this whiter than white.'

'Oh,' Tani said.

No wonder Kirstin had insisted on having the only room in the little house that overlooked Alys's dig, and anything that might go on there. The discovery of the stone casket must have seemed like a dream come true.

'Poor Heston.'

'Oh, I'm sure he'll recover. Might give him a chance to see what is right under his nose. Alys will do him the world of good. She's as sweet as can be, and with a backbone of iron. Once Kirstin's out of the way, I'm sure she'll work wonders.'

An arm began to steal around Tani's waist.

'Tani, I know this hasn't been the best of starts.'

'You can say that again.'

'I am going to have to disappear for a while, and it may be years before I can come back here.'

'I rather like it here,' Tani put in, with a smile.

'But I don't want to lose you.'

'Morris, just how long is this speech going to go on for?'

'Why?' he demanded. 'Am I boring you?'

'No. It's just I thought you might like to get to the end, and kiss me.'

'What did you just say?'

'Kiss me, you idiot.'

'And I thought you'd never ask.'

11

Bright spring sunshine sparked around the small boat taking Tani towards the nearest island. She looked around at the sunburned faces of the holidaymakers chattering excitedly, grasping their bags and their rucksacks, and their hordes of young children. She smiled.

'First time, love?' an elderly woman next to her enquired.

'Yes.'

'We come here every year, don't we, Harold?' she added to her husband snoozing gently at her side.

He gave a faint grunt, and returned to his slumbers.

'Different islands, of course. Never been disappointed. You have to see Greece in the spring, that's what I always say, while the flowers are still out. On your own, then?' the woman added, a faint hope in her voice of being able to take this pretty young woman under her wing, and show her the sights.

'Not exactly.'

Tani smiled at the well-meaning face.

'I'm not on holiday, you see. I've come to work.'

'That must be nice, dear. Hotel, is it?'

'No, at the temples. I'm an archaeological illustrator,' she explained.

'Really? How interesting. We love things like that, don't we, Harold? We were glued to that one that was on TV recently, the one that won all those awards, about a princess. Such a sad story. Did you see it, dear?'

'No, I didn't, I'm afraid. I've been working abroad a lot recently.'

'What a pity. It was lovely. I'm sure it will be repeated. They're making a new series for next year, they say.'

'Really?'

Tani was thankful the whitewashed buildings of the port were approaching rapidly, and the time for talking was over.

'I'll look out for it,' she added, with a smile.

It was a short taxi ride from the town to the ancient ruins of the temple, half hidden between olive groves and a bright splash of flowering meadows. The cheerful babble of voices talking away in various languages greeted her as the taxi driver lifted out her bags.

'I'm Tani, the illustrator,' she said, a little shyly, to the newly-sunburned young man who left his position scraping at the soil to greet her.

'Oh, hi,' he replied. 'We've been expecting you.'

He shouldered one of the bags, and set off.

'The professor's house is just up here.'

They walked through the olive trees to a tiny, whitewashed house with blue shutters.

'Come in!' was yelled from within, as her guide rapped on the door.

Tani stepped into the cool darkness, blinking as her eyes slowly adjusted from the brilliance outside.

'You're early,' the occupant remarked, seated at a large table covered in plans and maps, dressed only in shorts, an unbuttoned shirt and a dusty pair of sandals, pouring tea with one hand, a pencil gripped absently between his teeth.

'I managed to get an earlier flight, after all,' Tani replied.

She was aware of her guide watching the two of them with undisguised curiosity.

'I hope you don't mind.'

'Hey, no, great. We'd have sent someone to meet you from the boat, that's all.'

'That's OK,' Tani replied. 'I was told Greek taxis are the experience of a lifetime. I couldn't miss that, now, could I?'

The pencil was removed in time to prevent serious damage as its owner laughed.

'I'm quite sure,' he returned. 'Thanks, Tom. I'll bring Tani down to meet every-one in a bit.'

Tom retreated, with obvious regret. As he vanished between the trees Tani rubbed her tired eyes.

'Great start. I just didn't think what it might look like. I didn't mean to embarrass you.'

'Come here.'

'I'm hot, smelly and disgusting,' she protested.

'See if I care,' the reply came, and before she could move, she was enveloped in strong arms, and being kissed mercilessly. 'I've missed you,' he said at last, releasing her.

'Me, too,' she replied, winding her arms tightly around him.

They remained for a moment in contented silence. At last Tani raised her head.

'Morris.'

'Oh-oh, what have I done this time?'

'You might well ask. Tom was giving such strange looks while he was bringing me up here. Whatever have you been telling them about me?'

'Nothing.'

He gave her a sudden grin.

'I don't think they expected you to look like, well, you. He's probably wondering how this boring, old archaeology professor managed to get himself such a gorgeous wife. I expect they'll all be coming to me for tips all summer.'

'Morris, you're hopeless.'

She laughed and dodged as the arms threatened to tighten around her again.

'I brought some things for you.'

'They can wait.'

'No, they can't.'

'But I haven't seen you for nearly three weeks.'

'Well, it's up to you, of course, but it does include a package from Heston.'

'Ah, well, perhaps, in that case.'

Tani smiled, reached into her shoulder pack and handed him a large envelope.

'Alys sends her love, and said to tell you she's on to Plan B, whatever that is.'

Morris began to laugh.

'Just a few tips, that's all.'

'Tips?' Tani asked, looking puzzled.

'Yes. After all, I am one of Heston's oldest friends. I know all his little weaknesses. Who better to give pointers to love-lorn young females.'

'Morris, you're quite a disgrace,' Tani interrupted hastily. 'So is there a Plan C?'

'Of course, but that, my dear, is not at all for the ears of well-brought up females. Might give them no end of ideas. Mind you, on the other hand . . . '

'Idiot,' she replied, stifling a giggle.

'Heston is bound to see the light in the end. He was looking very thoughtful while we were waiting for you at the church, and don't tell me you didn't aim that bouquet straight at your bridesmaid for nothing.'

'Well, all right, maybe.'

'You'll see. They'll have babies screaming the place down by the time we get back.'

He pulled out a sheaf of documents, and a set of large photographs.

'Will you look at that!' he whistled. 'Beautiful.'

The photographs showed the carvings of animals and flowers that went all the way around the casket from Alys's trench.

'He's sent me some over the Internet, but nothing as detailed as this. I envied you going back to do the illustrations for the next TV series. It almost makes me wish . . . '

Tani leaned over him, looking over his shoulder at the photographs, her chin on the warm flesh, her arms draped around him.

'This isn't for ever, Morris.'

'I know, and I'm not complaining. I wouldn't miss the chance to be here for the world.'

'And at least Heston is speaking to you again.'

'Yes.'

His tone was somewhat dubious.

'Morris?'

'Yes, Mrs Professor?'

'Morris, what have you been up to now?'

'Nothing, at least, not much. You

know the bones they found in the casket?'

'Don't tell me you faked the DNA tests, and the man they found wasn't any relation to the prince at all.'

'Oh, no, nothing of the sort. Heston's right. It probably is the brother in there. It was just they found another skeleton in there, too. I just suggested to Alys that she should run a few tests.'

'And?'

'They showed that the skeleton was that of a woman who had lived most of her early life in the Mediterranean area. Alys e-mailed me yesterday. It kind of changes things, a bit.'

'Oh, you mean, the prince must have allowed Theodesa to be buried with her lover, after she died of a broken heart.' Tani frowned. 'But the tombstone, the one in the museum . . . '

'That could have been done any time. They didn't wait until you were dead to make those things, they took too long. That one could have been made before Prince Estyn had ever seen her. If it comes to it, it might not be anything to do with the real Ivory Princess at all.'

Tani digested this.

'Well, it does make a rather sweet end to the story, but it means I'll have to change one or two of my paintings.'

'Not exactly,' Morris said.

'What d'you mean?'

'Well, not exactly one or two. More like three or four or more, perhaps.'

'Morris, do you intend to spend the rest of your life tormenting me?'

'If it brings that particular colour to your cheeks, yes.'

'Morris!'

'Look, I only suggested Alys look in a certain direction because of the stories my grandmother used to tell. I'd given them up as fairy tales long ago. I never dreamed for a moment they might rise again to mess up Heston's precious museum. You see, in my grandmother's version, the moment they arrived at the castle, Prince Estyn's brother confessed that he and Theodesa had fallen madly in love, but when Prince Estyn threw him into prison with dire threats, the princess didn't lift a finger, and agreed to marry the prince, no messing.'

'But that's horrible!'

'Ah, but the next day when they came to collect her to go to church, they found she'd climbed out of the window, got back to her ship, and said that either Prince Estyn released his brother, or she was taking all her gold to his rival on the next headland, who'd probably use it to blast the castle to kingdom come. Come to think of it, you two would probably have got on like a house on fire.'

'So did she get her way?' Tani prompted.

'Mm? Oh, of course. I told you, you two have a lot in common. According to my grandmother, Prince Estyn declared that if that was what wives were like, he'd rather do without, thank you very much. So he handed over everything to his brother, and spent his life building monasteries. The earthquake probably happened centuries later, and just got mixed up with the story, like these things do, which brings us back to this casket, and the really bad news.'

'Yes?'

'Well, the bad news as far as Heston is concerned. You see, when Alys studied them more closely, she found that both skeletons in the casket were of people in their sixties, at least. People didn't live so long then, so that would be like getting your telegram from the Queen nowadays.'

Tani leaned forwards, laying her cheek against his, as she inspected the photographs in his hand. Every detail of the carvings danced with life, from the riotous winding of leaves and flowers, to the small animals, and the birds stealing fruit from between the branches. She had never, Tani thought suddenly, seen anything that so expressed a complete love of life, and of lives intertwined in perfect happiness.

'I like the idea,' she said, 'even if it

doesn't make for quite such a good story.'

'Me, too.'

Morris let the pictures rest on the table, and turned so that his face was very close to hers.

'We'll never know for certain,' he said, between slow and gentle kisses, 'not after all this time.'

He smiled, and pulled her closer.

'The only thing is, I don't know who is going to have the courage to break it to Heston that in his next TV series he might have to confess that it looks like the Ivory Princess lived happily every after, after all, just as we are going to, believe me.'

THE END

We do hope that you have enjoyed reading this large print book.

Did you know that all of our titles are available for purchase?

We publish a wide range of high quality large print books including:
Romances, Mysteries, Classics
General Fiction
Non Fiction and Westerns

Special interest titles available in large print are:
The Little Oxford Dictionary
Music Book, Song Book
Hymn Book, Service Book

Also available from us courtesy of Oxford University Press:
Young Readers' Dictionary
(large print edition)
Young Readers' Thesaurus
(large print edition)

For further information or a free brochure, please contact us at:
Ulverscroft Large Print Books Ltd.,
The Green, Bradgate Road, Anstey,
Leicester, LE7 7FU, England.
Tel: (00 44) **0116 236 4325**
Fax: (00 44) **0116 234 0205**

THE DOCTOR WAS A DOLL

Claire Vernon

Jackie runs a riding-school and, living happily with her father, feels no desire to get married. When Dr. Simon Hanson comes to the town, Jackie's friends try to matchmake, but he, like Jackie, wishes to remain single and they become good friends. When Jackie's father decides to remarry, she feels she is left all alone, not knowing the happiness that is waiting around the corner.

TO BE WITH YOU

Audrey Weigh

Heather, the proud owner of a small bus line, loves the countryside in her corner of Tasmania. Her life begins to change when two new men move into the area. Colin's charm overcomes her first resistance, while Grant also proves a warmer person than expected. But Colin is jealous when Grant gains special attention. The final test comes with the prospect of living in Hobart. Could Heather bear to leave her home and her business to be with the man she loves?

FINGALA, MAID OF RATHAY

Mary Cummins

On his deathbed, Sir James Montgomery of Rathay asks his daughter, Fingala, to swear that she will not honour her marriage contract until her brother Patrick, the new heir, returns from serving the King. Patrick must marry. Rathay must not be left without a mistress. But Patrick has fallen in love with the Lady Catherine Gordon whom the King, James IV, has given in marriage to the young man who claims to be Richard of York, one of the princes in the Tower.

ZABILLET OF THE SNOW

Catherine Darby

For Zabillet, a young peasant girl growing up in the tiny French village of Fromage in the mid-fourteenth century, a respectable marriage is the height of her parents' ambitions for her. But life is changing. Zabillet's love for a handsome shepherd is tested when she is invited to join the La Neige household, where her mistress, Lady Petronella, has plans for her grandson, Benet. And over all broods the horror of the Great Death that claims all whom it touches.